HOMETOWN HEARTS

Daddy Protector

USA TODAY Bestselling Author

JACQUELINE DIAMOND

Recycling programs for this product may not exist in your area.

ISBN-13: 978-0-373-21471-6

Daddy Protector

This edition published by arrangement with Harlequin Books S.A.

For questions and comments about the quality of this book, please contact us at CustomerService@Harlequin.com.

Printed in U.S.A.

Medical themes play a prominent role in many of **Jacqueline Diamond**'s one hundred published novels, including her Safe Harbor Medical miniseries for Harlequin American Romance. Her father was a small-town doctor before becoming a psychiatrist, and Jackie developed an interest in fertility issues after successfully undergoing treatment to have her two sons. A former Associated Press reporter and TV columnist, Jackie lives with her husband of thirty-seven years in Orange County, California, where she's active in Romance Writers of America. You can sign up for her free newsletter at jacquelinediamond.com and say hello to Jackie on her Facebook page, JacquelineDiamondAuthor. On Twitter, she's @jacquediamond.

To Beverley Sotolov and Jennifer Green.

HOMETOWN HEARTS

SHIPMENT 1

Stranger in Town by Brenda Novak
Baby's First Homecoming by Cathy McDavid
Her Surprise Hero by Abby Gaines
A Mother's Homecoming by Tanya Michaels
A Firefighter in the Family by Trish Milburn
Tempted by a Texan by Mindy Neff

SHIPMENT 2

It Takes a Family by Victoria Pade
The Sheriff of Heartbreak County by Kathleen Creighton
A Hometown Boy by Janice Kay Johnson
The Renegade Cowboy Returns by Tina Leonard
Unexpected Bride by Lisa Childs
Accidental Hero by Loralee Lillibridge

SHIPMENT 3

An Unlikely Mommy by Tanya Michaels
Single Dad Sheriff by Lisa Childs
In Protective Custody by Beth Cornelison
Cowboy to the Rescue by Trish Milburn
The Ranch She Left Behind by Kathleen O'Brien
Most Wanted Woman by Maggie Price
A Weaver Wedding by Allison Leigh

SHIPMENT 4

A Better Man by Emilie Rose
Daddy Protector by Jacqueline Diamond
The Road to Bayou Bridge by Liz Talley
Fully Engaged by Catherine Mann
The Cowboy's Secret Son by Trish Milburn
A Husband's Watch by Karen Templeton

SHIPMENT 5

His Best Friend's Baby by Molly O'Keefe
Caleb's Bride by Wendy Warren
Her Sister's Secret Life by Pamela Toth
Lori's Little Secret by Christine Rimmer
High-Stakes Bride by Fiona Brand
Hometown Honey by Kara Lennox

SHIPMENT 6

Reining in the Rancher by Karen Templeton
A Man to Rely On by Cindi Myers
Your Ranch or Mine? by Cindy Kirk
Mother in Training by Marie Ferrarella
A Baby for the Bachelor by Victoria Pade
The One She Left Behind by Kristi Gold
Her Son's Hero by Vicki Essex

SHIPMENT 7

Once and Again by Brenda Harlen
Her Sister's Fiancé by Teresa Hill
Family at Stake by Molly O'Keefe
Adding Up to Marriage by Karen Templeton
Bachelor Dad by Roxann Delaney
It's That Time of Year by Christine Wenger

SHIPMENT 8

The Rancher's Christmas Princess by Christine Rimmer
Their Baby Miracle by Lillian Darcy
Mad About Max by Penny McCusker
No Ordinary Joe by Michelle Celmer
The Soldier's Baby Bargain by Beth Kery
The Maverick's Christmas Baby by Victoria Pade

Chapter One

Hale Crandall really ought to put on some clothes. He looked fantastic without them, though, in Connie's opinion.

Sweat spread a bronze sheen across his rugged chest and face, from which exertion had stripped the customary know-it-all grin. A fierce, driving leap...breath coming hard... intensity turning his brown eyes to near-black...

Then he missed the softball, stumbled across the grass from his yard and plowed headfirst into the pansies and marigolds in Connie's flower bed. As she drove up, her amusement mutated into annoyance at her havoc-wreaking neighbor.

Muttering under her breath, she pulled her maroon sedan into the driveway and stomped on the brake. She yanked the door handle too hard, resulting in a chipped fingernail. Well, great! Not exactly Hale's fault, but she felt even more irked at him, anyway.

As she marched along the sidewalk—no sense ruining her strappy high heels or her lawn by taking the shortest route—she ignored the group of boys, assorted ages and states of griminess, who'd stopped playing to check on their ringleader. Why weren't they spending a Saturday in June doing something useful, like studying? Although Connie didn't have any children, she volunteered to tutor kids struggling in school, and knew how many of them blew off their assignments.

She stopped a few feet away from her neighbor. "Look at this mess! I hope you plan to replant those flowers." She barely refrained from adding a well-deserved, "You idiot!"

A dirt-smeared Hale pushed himself onto the grass and retrieved a clot of nasturtiums from atop his thick, dark hair. "Yes, ma'am," he replied with his customary sardonic edge.

With his taste for high jinks, she thought he might plant stinkweeds. "When you're buying the plants, be sure to get the same colors and varieties," she said. "It's the least you can do."

Rising, Hale dusted himself off. "I'll have my butler make a note." One of the boys giggled.

"Don't get smart with me!"

"Wouldn't dream of it."

As he turned away, Connie tried not to stare at his well-muscled bare back. Sure, Hale Crandall was one fine specimen of masculinity. Unfortunately, in her book, that too often meant thickheaded and irresponsible.

The problem was his resemblance to her ex-husband, Joel, Hale's best friend and fellow cop at the Villazon, California, Police Department. Together, the two overgrown adolescents had contributed to the breakup of her marriage. The only thing she'd snagged from the wreckage had been a pitiful monthly alimony check and this house—right next to Hale's.

"Hey, guys. Game's over!" As he headed for the porch, Hale waggled one hand at his followers, who dispersed reluctantly.

Connie retrieved her purse from the car. She had only an hour to grab an early dinner before returning to the gift shop she owned, since she'd agreed to let Jo Anne Larouche, her clerk, leave at five for personal reasons.

Her mother would have scolded Connie for being too soft on an employee. But in her opinion, treating workers well kept them loyal. And she was willing to work long hours if that's what success required.

From the corner of her eye, she glimpsed a straggler trailing into Hale's house, a wiry little boy with blond hair. Darned if he didn't bear a strong resemblance to Skip Enright, the six-year-old she tutored at the town's homework center. Co-founded by a retired teacher and by a close friend of Connie's, the afterschool-and-weekend operation used volunteers to help kids master reading and math.

Just before the boy disappeared indoors, a cobalt gleam flashed from the heels of his running shoes. She'd bought Skip a pair exactly like those to celebrate his successful completion of first grade. Not only were they expensive, but she'd found them during a buying trip to L.A. That left no doubt in her mind about his identity.

Between the boy's independent spirit and his foster mother's preoccupation with the pending birth of a grandchild, he roamed far too freely around town. Anxious to provide sorely lacking supervision, Connie had brought Skip home several afternoons with the permission of his foster mother. If he'd wandered this way in search of her today, then she'd better retrieve him and drive him home.

To avoid any more contact with her neighbor than necessary, she took out her cell phone and dialed Hale's number. Once he learned about the little intruder, he'd likely send the kid straight out.

A machine picked up. Why didn't the man answer? And he refused to provide the number of his cell. Probably he didn't care to listen to her complain whenever he threw one of his loud parties, Connie admitted, but still…

She glared at his ranch-style home. Even under the best of circumstances, she disliked setting foot inside it. Too many uncomfortable memories from when her husband used to hang out there. Come to think of it, there were no best circumstances.

Marching along the walkway, she tried to ignore the weeds peeping through the cracks and the brown fronds dangling from an overgrown bird-of-paradise plant. At the top of the steps, she pressed the bell twice, waited and then knocked loudly. Zilch.

Being ignored had never stopped her before when she had a bone of contention with her neighbor, and it wouldn't prevent her now from collecting the boy to whom she'd grown so attached.

Turning the knob, she went in, hit by the lingering smell of cigarette and cigar smoke. Although Hale didn't indulge, his guests obviously did.

A billiards table dominated the living room amid mismatched chairs and a couch. On the walls, motorcycle posters reinforced the pool-hall theme. A crumpled potato chip bag lay in one corner.

She passed a den dominated by a vast TV screen and videogame system, and reached the kitchen. Skip was perched at the kitchen counter munching what appeared to be cheese puffs. Above him, doorless cabinets revealed a tooth-rotting supply of cookies and chips. Simply allowing a youngster in this kitchen ought to count as child abuse!

Hale, his head in the kitchen sink as he sprayed water over his upper body, either didn't notice the boy or didn't mind. Averting her eyes from the masculine figure, Connie addressed Skip. "Hi, fella. What brings you here?"

The boy grinned. "Cool place, huh?"

"If you say so." Despite the possible damage to her suit from his soiled clothing, she gave him a hug.

The half-naked host switched off the water, grabbed a frayed towel from the counter and rubbed his hair as he swung around. Moisture beaded on bare flesh…as if Connie cared!

Only a slight hesitation betrayed his reaction on spotting her. “Aha. The princess braves the ogre’s lair.”

“Are you aware that this little boy followed you inside?” she demanded.

“I may be stupid but I’m not blind.” He seemed to take pride in ducking the issue.

Irked, Connie continued, “Didn’t it occur to you to find out where he belongs?”

The towel draped across his bare shoulders, Hale regarded her with feigned innocence. “Hey, he’s a guy. Why can’t he just hang out?” He tossed a handful of cheese puffs one by one into the air and caught them in his mouth. Missed one, picked it up and ate it anyway.

“Hale…”

“Okay, okay,” he said. “A lady named Paula was trying to drop him off at your place. I said he could stay here ’til you showed up.”

That would be Paula Layton, Skip’s foster mother. Apparently she hadn’t bothered to call. “She left him with a complete stranger?”

That was scary. Just because someone lived next door didn't make him trustworthy.

"She saw my picture in the paper last year when I got a commendation." Hale had been honored for recognizing an L.A. robbery suspect at the supermarket. He'd quietly called for backup and trailed the man outside to collar him without endangering shoppers. "What can I say? I stick in some people's minds."

"Like a piece of chewing gum on their shoe," Connie mocked. Of course, she'd been impressed by Hale's actions, too, but admitting as much would only give him an advantage in their ongoing game of one-upmanship.

Skip seemed to find her remark funny. His laughter bubbled up, wonderfully free and open. He retained a warm spirit, despite a history of neglect that included removal from his birth home after neighbors repeatedly called social services about his lack of supervision. He'd been returned to his parents briefly, until their arrest for selling drugs. Eventually they'd agreed to relinquish custody.

"The kid's been here about an hour," Hale added. "This Paula person said her daughter was in labor and she had to rush off to the hospital. She wasn't sure but he might have to stay overnight."

"She might have phoned!" Connie wondered what the woman would have done with Skip if Hale hadn't been available. "I understand her desire to be at the hospital, but she could have made babysitting arrangements. Her daughter's full-term, so this hardly comes as a surprise."

The real problem wasn't today's drop-off but Paula's increasing inattentiveness to her ward. With a grandchild on the way, the woman seemed to have lost the motivation that had inspired her to begin foster parenting in the first place.

As his foster mom became emotionally detached, Connie became more attached to Skip. Maybe he'd awakened her long-dormant maternal instincts. Maybe his personality, combined with the approach of her thirtieth birthday, had done the trick, but regardless of the reason, she'd grown to love him. And from there, an impulse to provide him with a home had developed into a powerful longing.

Foster parents had priority in an adoption. However, in response to Connie's inquiry, Paula, whose married daughter had then just announced her pregnancy, had conceded that she might be willing to give him up. To learn whether she'd be allowed to adopt as a single parent, Connie had consulted a lawyer. He'd explained that school-age children were hard to place compared to infants and toddlers, and someone like her who'd already formed a connection with Skip ought to encounter no problems.

She'd applied to adopt and undergone the required home study. Then, to her disappointment, Paula had changed her mind. Her grandchild-to-be was a girl, and her husband liked having a boy around. Yet however sincere Mr. Layton's interest, the trucker spent weeks at a stretch on the road.

Still, Paula's lackadaisical style hadn't quite crossed the gap into negligence, and her opposition would doom any attempt to gain permanent custody. Since Connie couldn't afford a legal battle and wasn't sure she'd win, anyway, she simply did her best to provide support.

"Okay if I take you to the store with me for a couple of hours?" she asked Skip. She maintained a stash of toys to occupy customers' children.

"Sure!"

Connie removed the snack bag and rolled it shut. "Let's eat at my place. Frozen dinners okay?" She hoped he liked fish or chicken. Those were all she'd stocked.

"Cool!"

Hale tugged an old T-shirt over his head. Clinging to his damp torso, it revealed almost as much as it hid. "I'd offer to watch him myself if I didn't have plans for the evening."

"You've done plenty already." The boy needed stability and order. The less contact he had with this man, the better, in Connie's opinion. "Thanks for filling in."

"No problem." He flashed a teasing smile. "I'll stop by a garden center tomorrow and pick out your posies. Nothing I enjoy more than spending a Sunday afternoon digging in the dirt, getting back to my ancestral roots as a farmer."

Under the circumstances, Connie decided not to comment on the greater likelihood that he'd descended from some notorious scoundrel. "I'd appreciate it."

She shepherded Skip out of the house, her mind racing. There was barely time to call Paula and explain that they'd be at the shop—as if the woman gave the boy a second thought!—and to heat the dinners.

As she opened her door, she recalled Hale's mention of plans for the evening. Those probably involved one of the women she occasionally glimpsed on his property or whose voices drifted over the wall from the swimming pool. His female interests always appeared to have great fun, but as far as Connie could tell, none of them lasted long.

Well, the man's love life didn't concern her. The two of them moved in entirely different spheres, and she meant to keep it that way. No matter how terrific he looked without his shirt.

Hale fished out another handful of cheese puffs. The party at the captain's place didn't start for an hour and he was hungry. Perhaps he should have insinuated his way over to Connie's for one of those frozen dinners.

Bad idea. He grimaced at the memory of plunging into her flower bed. Why couldn't she be satisfied with just grass? As for her house, a man couldn't swing his arms without upending half a dozen china or glass doodads.

Noticing cheese crud on his T-shirt, Hale stared down in displeasure. Oh, well, he had to change into fancy duds in a few minutes, anyway, to mingle with the upper crust at the gathering.

Villazon's relatively new police chief, Willard Lyons, encouraged his brass and detectives to hobnob with the town's leaders. In view of the police department's image problems—there'd been a couple of scandals—tonight's cocktail party hosted by Captain Frank Ferguson counted more as public relations than as entertainment.

Much better to spend the evening tossing back beers with a few buddies, or even better… Wait! Wait! Hale tried to short-circuit the scenario that sprang to mind. No use. In his king-size bed lounged Connie Simmons, blond hair spread across the pillow and luscious breasts threatening to burst from beneath the sheets. Lips parted, waiting breathlessly for him to peel away the covers.

A cheese puff slipped through his fingers, this time straight to the floor, which already cried out for sweeping. Hale stared downward, still tantalized by his vision.

He couldn't fathom why his fantasies never quite revealed Connie's nudity, since he'd been drawn to her ever since his buddy Joel had introduced the sensual beauty seven or eight years ago. Instead of being an only child, why couldn't he have sisters who brought home friends like that? If he'd gotten to her first, well, no guarantees about anything long-term, but for sure he'd have satisfied his curiosity.

Grumbling under his breath, Hale went on a hunt for the vacuum cleaner. Must have loaned it to somebody. Unable to find a broom, either, he got down on his hands and knees and used his hands to scrape the kitchen detritus into a pile, which he then pushed onto a spatula.

The activity must have restored function to his rational side, because he recognized at last why he couldn't bring himself to picture Connie's tantalizing hidden body parts. *Because it would be like cheating on my pal.*

He and Joel had survived a lot together, including virtual outcast status two years ago when Joel was forced to testify against a lieutenant and the department's then-chief, Vince Borrego, about their misconduct. The stress had made Joel touchy, for which Connie, still married to Joel, perversely blamed Hale. Easier than accepting the fact that she hadn't stood by her husband when he needed her.

That might be another reason Hale didn't allow his daydreams to get too…intimate. Even under the best of conditions, serving on a police force took a heavy toll on relationships. Why waste the effort on a woman who'd already demonstrated an inability to stay the course?

Except that, in the matter of Hale's taste in

women, she fit like a key in a door. The door to the bedroom.

He stuffed the empty bag into the trash, then sauntered toward the hall, stopping to pluck a couple of darts off the sofa and stick them into the dartboard. In the master bedroom, Hale drew the curtains on the side facing Connie's house. The fact that his window lay directly opposite hers forced them both to be extra careful about privacy.

He'd ordered the heaviest drapes he could find. Black velvet, to match the black satin sheets. Hale took pride in having coordinated at least part of his decor, not that Connie would ever witness it.

Rinsing off in the kitchen hadn't satisfied him, so he showered, shaved, dashed on cologne and wrestled with a shirt, suit and tie. Might as well get a bit more use out of the outfit he'd bought last month for Officer Rachel Byers's wedding.

Rachel was one of Connie's closest friends, as well as a buddy of Hale's. She'd married the town's new pediatrician, Dr. Russ McKenzie, at the Villazon Community Church. Big affair, with the entire police department invited, and a blast afterward at the Villa Inn.

Weddings were great fun, as long as they were someone else's.

Hale was striding toward the garage when he spotted Skip's small duffel bag atop the washing machine. He'd forgotten setting it there after the boy arrived.

A peek inside revealed pajamas printed with cartoon characters. A toothbrush and a couple of toys were tucked underneath. A safe bet the kid would go to bed before Hale made it home.

Returning this stuff meant confronting the dragon lady once more. With a shrug, he let himself out through the garage and spared a longing glance at the motorcycle and all-terrain vehicle he hadn't had a chance to ride in ages.

At the next house, Connie's maroon sedan was gone. A wisp of memory flashed through his mind as he stared at the empty driveway: her blond hair caught in the breeze as she zoomed up and parked the red convertible she used to drive. Joel, tuning his car in the garage, had ignored his wife's struggle with sacks of groceries. Marriage did that to a guy, Hale supposed. Turned him blind, deaf and really, really dumb.

Which was kind of how he felt, standing

on the porch ringing the bell when he knew nobody would answer. He supposed he could drop the duffel on her rear porch with a note. But Connie's Curios was on the way to Frank's house, and besides, Skip might want his toys.

A visit to the gift shop. Since he'd never set foot inside, this ought to prove interesting.

Hale tooled through the neighborhood past fallen lavender blooms that mirrored the cloudlike shapes of jacaranda trees. A short distance beyond the residential area, a strip mall featured a discount furniture store, a supermarket, the storefront office of the weekly *Villazon Voice,* and at the corner of the intersection with Arches Avenue, Connie's Curios. Its red-and-white exterior framed a lacy window display bearing the banner "Welcome June Brides."

In the parking area, the thin sprinkling of cars gave the place an isolated air. On a weekend, the small office building around the corner and behind the gift store didn't generate much traffic, either.

Connie should rethink her policy of staying open 'til seven on Fridays and Saturdays. That was only an hour later than usual, but it *felt* late.

As a cop, Hale knew that Villazon, situated

on the eastern rim of Los Angeles County adjacent to Orange County, had a low crime rate. But no telling who might wander into Connie's Curios looking for a till full of cash.

Joel had disagreed with his wife's decision to go into business, Hale recalled. She'd insisted she had the right, since she was investing half of an inheritance from her grandparents in it, but he'd have preferred to buy a vacation cabin. If her safety had been a concern, though, Joel hadn't mentioned it. Since he'd already blown the other half of her inheritance on a bad investment entered into without Connie's agreement, Joel had reluctantly backed down.

Hale stepped inside to the accompaniment of chimes. The swirl of pinks, reds and lavenders and the array of frilly merchandise made him feel dizzy. Who on earth bought this many greeting cards, stuffed animals, china bells and figurines, mugs, T-shirts, pens, magnets, clocks, key chains, puzzles, scrapbooks and candles? Not to mention comic books, animal characters and action figures.

Still, a fellow could go for the bins of wrapped candies and racks of Swiss and Italian chocolate bars. Might be worth springing for one, except he'd probably arrive at the captain's house with a smear of chocolate on his tie.

From behind the counter, Connie regarded him frostily. "Something I can do for you, Detective?"

Sure, lots of things. But none of them in public. "Thought you might have some use for this." Hale swung the duffel onto the counter, dislodging a catalog showing gift baskets. "It belongs to Skip. Where is the little guy?"

She indicated a children's nook where, ensconced in a beanbag chair, the boy was absorbed in watching a shiny red TV set. "He got tired of helping me count change."

Hale whistled. "I didn't expect a store like this to carry electronics."

"We offer specialty items tailored for kids. Grandparents get a kick out of them. We have gadgets for adults, as well." Connie appeared to warm to her subject.

"Where do you find stuff like that?" Since the items she stocked bore little resemblance to the products in ordinary stores, Hale supposed she must have special sources.

"Catalogs, sales reps, the internet and specialty trade shows in Anaheim and L.A." Both convention centers lay within a forty-five-minute drive.

So far, no customers had entered, and he'd observed none when he arrived. "You earn a living at this?"

Although her forehead puckered, Connie didn't fling a retort. "There's a thin margin of profit, but yes. I'm always bringing in new merchandise, so people drop by frequently, and we have regular customers who collect specialty items. Also, I coordinate with party and wedding planners, arrange craft classes and maintain gift registries. Plus, we do about forty percent of our business in November and December."

"You carry the same stuff at your other stores?" Connie owned the concession at the hospital and a boutique in the town's funky shopping mart, In a Pickle, which occupied the site of a former pickling plant.

"Each one is unique." She spoke with uncharacteristic patience. "I encourage my managers to imprint their personality and cater to their clientele. So you'll find a lot of food items and Latin American imports at the Pickle, and flowers, books and magazines at the medical center."

Hale had run out of questions. Wanted to keep her talking, though. Maybe he felt a little protective, seeing her here alone on a Saturday evening. And the cozy scents of cinnamon and peppermint hinted at a childhood he barely remembered. Also, he wasn't too keen on the dull evening ahead.

"So are you planning any more—" Hale halted at a peculiar scraping noise from the back of the store.

Connie shifted uneasily. "Sounds like someone's in the storage room. Or it could be an animal, I suppose. A cat might have sneaked in from the alley."

Hale kept his voice low. "How about an employee?"

A headshake. "Jo Anne left a while ago." Her fists tightened atop the counter. "We had a break-in attempt from the alley a few nights ago after hours. The alarm scared off whoever it was."

He reached into his jacket for the holstered gun he always carried. "You leave the back unlocked during working hours?"

"No, but Jo Anne put out the trash. Maybe she forgot to lock up."

"Who else has a key?"

"Just Jo Anne." She gave a little cough before continuing. "She wouldn't enter that way without letting me know." She shot a glance at Skip, who remained fixed on the TV screen.

Through the glass front, the parking lot appeared as sparsely occupied as when Hale had arrived. No sign of trouble there.

"I'll check it out." He pointed the gun's barrel toward the floor. "Might be a rodent or some merchandise falling over."

"Let's hope…" Connie halted at another noise from the storeroom. It sounded to Hale like the scuff of a shoe.

"Call 911," he ordered tensely. "Stay low behind the counter, out of the line of fire. Leave Skip where he is." There was no time. Someone might burst out at any second.

Connie reached for the phone. No hysterics or nonsense. Hale appreciated that.

Raising the gun, he approached the rear door at an angle, kicked it open, shouted, "Police! Come out with your hands up!" and braced for action.

Chapter Two

Credit card fraud. Shoplifting. Vandalism and burglary. They were all issues Connie had prepared for when she opened a shop. The classes she'd taken had even instructed her how to handle a break-in: "Don't keep much money in the till. If a robber demands it, give him everything on hand."

But a furtive intruder from the alley, on a Saturday night when she might have been the only adult present? Terrifying.

She forced herself to breathe steadily as she provided the dispatcher with her name and location. "I think someone's broken into my storeroom. An off-duty officer is checking it out. Hale Crandall. He requested backup."

"I'm sending it now," the woman responded. "Please stay on the line."

No one had responded to Hale's verbal challenge. Instead, she'd heard a scuffling noise as if the intruder was retreating.

After a split second, Hale had gone after him. Typical testosterone-infused male, running an unnecessary risk, except that, perversely, Connie admired the heck out of him for doing it. Much as she normally preferred standing on her own two feet, she felt a surge of gratitude for Hale. Certainly not an emotion she usually associated with her neighbor.

As a siren wailed in the distance, Connie wondered what was happening out of her sight. She thought she heard men speaking in the alley, or was that the TV?

Across the shop, Skip got up and trotted between the displays to join her. "Where'd Hale go, Connie?"

"We heard a noise," she told him.

"Wow! I saw his gun!" He beamed, too young to grasp that his new friend might get killed. But Connie remained all too aware of the danger.

For the three years of her marriage, she'd

lived with the fear of a knock at the door and the news that Joel was dead or wounded, and she'd vowed never to forget that life was fragile. But she'd never once worried about Hale. A moment before, he'd stood in front of her, tall and cheerful and seemingly indestructible. Now she might lose him, and that possibility scared her more than she would have expected. A lot more.

She heard footsteps coming through the storage room. A moment's tension, and then Hale called out, "Tell Dispatch to cancel the cavalry. I'm okay."

"Hale says everything's fine," she informed the woman on the phone.

"May I speak to him, please?"

He entered, grinning. The cocky expression gave Connie an urge to slap him for provoking such anxiety.

Behind him trailed a sheepish Vince Borrego, the town's former police chief who, since being forced to resign, had worked as a private investigator. His office lay across the alley in the building behind the shop, and he occasionally visited to pick up treats for his daughter and grandchildren.

She thrust out the phone to Hale. He stepped aside with it, leaving her to face the older man.

"Sorry for the ruckus." In his late fifties, Vince had a gravelly voice and deep wrinkles, souvenirs of his former heavy smoking and drinking. "I was leaving my office and noticed your rear door ajar. Decided to make sure nobody'd sneaked inside, but when Hale shouted a warning, it startled me. I've been trying to stay out of trouble, given my history in this town, so I skedaddled. Dumb move."

"Thanks for your concern. About the open door, I mean." Connie found it reassuring that the ex-chief had been looking out for her security.

"Glad to help."

In front, a police cruiser halted. Hale concluded his discussion with the dispatcher and went to consult with the officer.

"Hi, Vince!" Skip high-fived the older man, who lived in the same fourplex as the Laytons. Connie had bumped into him a few weeks earlier when she dropped her student off after a tutoring session, and discovered that she and Vince shared similar concerns about the boy.

"Good to see you, fella." To complete the greeting, Vince lightly slapped the little hand down low, as well as on high. "Got to get you together with my grandson. You're close to the same age."

"Cool!" With Connie's permission, the little boy chose a couple of hard candies and trotted back to the TV.

"What brings our little man to Connie's Curios?" Vince asked as he picked out several chocolate bars.

She explained about Paula's dropping him off at Hale's house. "I'm glad she didn't leave him alone in the apartment," he responded. "She does that on occasion, although usually for less than an hour."

"Even so, that's disturbing." When Connie had asked her lawyer about the matter, he'd explained that the law didn't specify a minimum age at which a child had to be supervised. Once children reached school age, authorities generally didn't crack down unless harm resulted.

Fortunately, the fourplex where Skip lived belonged to Yolanda Rios, co-founder of the homework center, and she helped keep an eye on the boy. It was she who'd discovered he was having problems in kindergarten the previous year and brought him in for tutoring.

"I talked to a lawyer about adopting. If Paula's not going to make a real home for him, I wish she'd give me a chance," Connie grumbled.

"You'd make a great mom," Vince was agreeing when Hale returned.

He broke stride, evidently having overheard the end of the conversation. "Did I miss something?"

"Nothing important." Vince paid for his purchases. "If things do work out, don't forget my daughter, Keri, has a home day care license."

"She's first on my list." Connie's friend Rachel, whose stepdaughter stayed with Keri after school, sang the woman's praises.

With a wary nod to both of them, the ex-chief exited. Hale stared at the man's retreating back. "What was that about?"

"Vince rents the apartment across the hall from Skip's. They're friends."

"Yeah, well, he seems awfully chummy with you. 'You'd make a great mom,'" Hale mimicked. "You haven't forgotten the guy's got wandering hands, have you?" Part of Vince's problems with the PD had involved his misconduct toward a female officer.

Connie couldn't decide whether to laugh or take offense. "He's never made a pass at me. Besides, he's too old."

"How old is too old to pursue younger women?" Hale scoffed. "Besides, why *was* he plying you with compliments?"

She curbed her temper by remembering that her neighbor had risked his neck to investigate the noises. Softly so the boy wouldn't hear, she replied, "He was responding to my statement that I'd like to adopt Skip."

"Gee, I guess you forgot to mention that to me. But of course everybody confides in Villazon's Grandpa of the Year, don't they?" Hale muttered.

How unfair! "You may find this hard to believe, but Vince has changed. He cares about people."

"What did he offer to do—plant incriminating evidence on Paula so she'd lose custody?" he cracked.

The remark undoubtedly reflected deep-seated anger at Vince and the painful impact he'd had on his colleagues. A few years earlier, Officer Elise Masterson had accused the then-chief of sexual harassment and named Joel as a witness—his job as a watch commander put him in a key position to observe departmental goings-on. Joel had also had to testify in a separate investigation into claims that a lieutenant had beaten a prisoner and that Vince had covered for him.

The department had endured a rough period, its reputation besmirched and the officers' loyalties divided, with many criticizing Joel for testifying. Hale had stood by him, and after the hiring of a new chief, the whole affair had blown over.

Vince had taken early retirement and the department fired the lieutenant, Norm Kinsey. Both had left the area until, six months ago, Vince moved back to be near his daughter.

On his visits to the shop, he seemed affable and courteous. In Connie's opinion, the ex-chief had learned a hard lesson from the loss of his career and the breakup of his marriage. It wasn't his fault that, a few months ago, he'd shot and killed a prison escapee who'd targeted his family, and news reports had rehashed the entire original scandal just as it was fading from the public's memory.

Plant evidence against Paula! How absurd. "He didn't offer to do anything of the sort."

"Take my advice and watch out for him," Hale answered dourly.

How could he be so paranoid? "You're being unreasonable," she said.

"Do me a favor and keep your guard up."

Before she could answer, Hale added, "You're seriously interested in adopting?"

She nodded. "Very much so."

He checked that Skip remained in his corner before asking, "Why a boy? You've got a house full of frilly stuff."

She was taken by surprise. "This isn't about choosing just any child! It's about Skip. Hale, we don't choose who we love."

He tugged at his tie. Whoever he was dating tonight, he must think highly of her to endure such discomfort. "The boy deserves a father figure."

"I grew up without a father, and I'm fine!"

That she'd grown up fatherless wasn't entirely true. Although Connie's parents had divorced when she was ten, Jim Lawson had lived nearby and remained theoretically involved. But Connie had never felt he'd played any meaningful role in her life.

The incident that stood out in her mind had occurred when she was fifteen and spending a weekend with him, her stepmother and their one-year-old son. On Saturday night, their babysitter had canceled at the last minute. Never mind that Connie was excited about attending a school dance with a new boyfriend;

her father had insisted that she stay home and fill in. He'd dismissed her tears as selfish.

Selfish! She still got mad thinking about it. If she'd had other, warmer memories of her dad, no doubt she'd have forgiven him. But she didn't.

"Yeah, well, I grew up without a mother, so between the two of us, we had an almost perfect childhood." Hale grinned, then added, "Before you adopt, though, remember that the great thing about other people's kids is, when you get tired of 'em, you can send 'em home."

"That's what I used to think, too," she admitted. "But people change. I've changed. Maybe you will, too, someday."

"Stranger things have happened." A slight concession, or perhaps simply a way of ducking the subject. "I'd better be going. Lock the back door first, okay?"

"Absolutely."

After she did so, he left via the front, passing a couple of teenage girls who ogled him blatantly. They giggled incessantly while picking out hair ornaments, and Connie suspected the subject was Hale.

She rang up their purchases, amused that her neighbor inspired so much girlish interest. He *had* been considerate to drop off Skip's bag.

And fiercely protective when he heard the noise in back. Remembering the tension in his dark eyes and the power in his movements gave her a twinge of longing. A zap of common sense followed on its heels.

The great thing about other people's kids is, when you get tired of 'em, you can send 'em home. She could hardly expect any other attitude from Hale. Vince Borrego might have reformed, but she doubted her playboy neighbor ever would. Too bad. He sometimes showed hints of potential for being a good man.

Connie went to switch off the video and collect Skip. She had enough love in her heart to make a home for this child if she was ever lucky enough to get the chance. That would be family enough, at least for now.

As usual on a Monday morning, Hale found his desk piled with reports from the weekend. His assignments in the Crimes Against Persons Unit ranged from missing persons to assaults. A small city like Villazon had mercifully few homicides but plenty of felonies, and he spent the morning reviewing crime-scene accounts and citizen complaints, following up on witnesses and conferring with other law-enforcement agencies whose cases overlapped his.

Recalling the adrenaline rush he'd experienced during the incident on Saturday at Connie's shop made him miss his years on patrol. Not that he didn't occasionally get to take down a suspect, but in his position as a detective, the paperwork drove him crazy.

Still, Hale enjoyed the challenge of discerning the facts and tracking down crooks. He supposed he ought to be studying for the exam to earn promotion to sergeant, which Joel had passed several years ago, but that might mean a transfer to a different division.

He didn't require extra income to pay alimony, either. Sipping his third—or maybe fourth—cup of coffee of the morning, Hale flexed the arm muscles he'd strained yesterday replanting Connie's flowers. Darn, that woman was bossy! But fun to tease, and kind of sweet once in a while.

Opening the first case file, he got to work. The hours vanished silently and swiftly, until the scream of sirens from the fire station next door jolted him from his absorption. "Chemical fire in a warehouse on the east side," noted Detective Lieutenant E. J. Corwin, who paused in striding toward his office.

A second siren blared. "What kind of chemicals?" Things could get ugly fast in any blaze, especially one that involved toxic substances. Firefighting was even more dangerous than police work, according to Hale's insurance agent.

"Unidentified."

Not a good sign. However, police usually only got involved with fires to control traffic. Or when bodies turned up, which he hoped didn't happen.

Thirty minutes later, as the idea of buying a sandwich from a vending machine loomed large in his mind, the phone rang. To his terse response, a woman said, "The chief would like to see you in his office, Hale." The voice belonged to Lois Lamont, the sixtyish secretary whose tenure dated back to the late Mesozoic era.

"I'm on my way." He rang off. He had no reason to expect trouble, but neither did he usually pal around with Willard Lyons.

The new chief had come on board the previous year to clean up the PD's image. At Saturday night's party, he'd glad-handed the community leaders and stayed until the bitter end, or at least as much of the bitter end as Hale had observed before bowing out at eleven.

The man worked hard, and according to office gossip, he'd had a reputation as a decent cop in his previous positions with the Whittier PD and LAPD. The guys respected him, even if no one felt particularly chummy. Will Lyons's manner didn't invite chumminess.

Hale walked past the watch commander's office and the traffic bureau, his curiosity growing with every step.

The secretary's desk and several file cabinets crammed the small outer office. When he entered, Lois peered at him through owlish glasses beneath a fuzzy orange halo of thinning hair. "None of your cheekiness today, young man. He's not in a good mood."

"*Moi?* Cheeky?" All the same, Hale appreciated the warning.

"I hope you haven't settled for any of the ladies in this town yet," Lois continued. "My beautiful nieces put them in the shade. You really ought to let me introduce you. They won't stay single forever."

She'd been offering to fix him up for years in what had evolved into a running joke. Judging by the photos on her desk, the girls seemed pretty enough but not Hale's type. *Not blonde and smart-mouthed with a quick temper.* "I'm married to my work," he said. "Haven't you noticed?"

She sighed, then indicated the inner door. "Go ahead."

Inside, light through a large window flooded the expansive office. The wooden desk and conference table from Vince's tenure had been refinished and the chairs reupholstered. Satellite images of Villazon hung where once the walls had displayed photos of the town's quaint former city hall.

"Close the door, please," the chief said.

Must be a sensitive subject. Curious and a bit wary, Hale obeyed and followed the chief's directive to take a seat.

With his broad chest, thin mustache and close-cropped brown hair, Will Lyons fit the image of a police administrator. Not merely a bureaucrat, though; more than once, he'd helped resolve an investigation by asking key questions of the detectives.

In his thirteen months on the job, not once had Lyons acted nervous or uncertain in Hale's presence. Now, however, he folded his hands atop the desk and cleared his throat.

The words "So what's bothering you, boss?" nearly slipped from Hale's lips. That's what he'd have said to Vince in the old days.

But no one joked freely with Chief Lyons and, besides, Lois's warning rang in his ears. So he waited.

Finally the chief said, "I'd like you to probe something discreetly. It may appear that I'm protecting myself, but the fact is, I think this may be an attempt to embarrass the department. If at any point you believe these contentions are true, Detective, you're to treat this as you would any other case."

Curiosity about the subject warred with an instinctive dislike of subterfuge. "Why me?" If this was a politically sensitive issue, he'd rather it went to someone of higher rank, such as Frank Ferguson, captain of the detective bureau and interim chief before Lyons's arrival.

"Because every man and woman on this force likes and respects you," his boss replied. "I'm a relative stranger here. If any of this comes out, they'll trust you to be absolutely honest."

Did his fellow officers respect him that much? As chief party animal, Hale knew he had friends. But if he was truly held in such high regard, it meant more than all the commendations he'd received over the years.

That kind of esteem, however, brought responsibility. "What exactly are you asking me to do?"

Lyons tapped a pad by his phone. "I received a troubling call this morning from Tracy Johnson at the newspaper."

The publisher, editor and reporter of the *Villazon Voice* pursued stories with a zeal that often scooped dailies and TV stations. She'd never given the police a break, but she was usually fair.

"What about?" Hale asked.

The chief released a long breath. "A source of Tracy's claims my son is dealing drugs."

Here was a potato hot enough to burn anyone who touched it, Hale mused. Which made it possible the chief had chosen him at least in part because, if anything went amiss, a lowly detective made a better scapegoat than a high-ranking officer.

The chief's nineteen-year-old son, Ben, had reputedly run wild since his mother's death from cancer five years earlier. He'd served a stint in juvenile detention for drug use and now participated in a treatment program. He also took classes at community college and delivered pizzas.

The young man and his strict father didn't

get along. Were barely speaking, according to the grapevine.

"She has no details and refuses to name her source," Lyons went on. "Since she can't prove anything, she volunteered the information in exchange for a promise that, whenever we have news to release, we give her a heads-up if possible."

"Big of her," Hale muttered.

"I didn't agree to an exclusive, only that we'd alert her." After a moment, the chief added, "She did say she hoped it isn't true."

"So do I." Okay, they had an unconfirmed report about drug dealing. "Shouldn't the narcs handle this?" Or perhaps an outside agency, given the potential conflict of interest.

Lyons stared out the window as if he'd developed a keen interest in the adjacent library. "You don't have children, do you?" Without pausing, he continued, "If I launch a formal investigation of my son based on rumor, he'll perceive that as a betrayal. I'd also be throwing him back into hot water, perhaps unfairly, just when he's starting to get his act together. It's not his fault that his dad's the police chief and everything that concerns me makes news. On the other hand, I can't ignore this."

"This drug program he's in, don't they monitor him?" Hale inquired.

"He finished the program two months ago." The chief refocused on his visitor. "He's on probation and I'm sure they test for drugs, so I really don't believe there's any truth to this."

"You've seen his place, right? Notice anything strange?"

The chief released a frustrated breath. "Ben doesn't care to have his old man around, so Frank did me the favor of dropping by a couple of times to see if he was okay. I gather my son didn't welcome him, but he did let him inside, and Frank saw nothing obviously amiss. So what do you say?"

Hale tried to decide what, as a towering figure of integrity, he ought to do. He decided to simply act like himself. Also, his gut told him that despite the polite phrasing, this was an assignment, not a request. "So I'm to sniff around and discover if there's any truth to it?"

"Exactly. His landlady's a retired teacher by the name of Yolanda Rios. She should be aware of the signs if he's dealing."

The kid lived in the same complex as Vince and Skip? Well, *there* was a coincidence. Still, in an area with a low vacancy rate, he'd heard that Yolanda preferred to rent to friends of friends, and it wasn't much of a stretch to imagine that both Vince and Ben had found their way to her through their connections in the community.

This could be fortunate. As the chief said, a former teacher ought to recognize the signs of a drug pusher, including frequent visitors at odd hours and higher spending than the person's income justified. Also, if Ben had resumed using, he would probably exhibit a glassy stare, mood swings and other symptoms.

"I took a history class from Mrs. Rios once. Great teacher," Hale noted. "She has a fondness for strays, but she'd never tolerate drugs." An interesting possibility occurred to him. "I have an idea where that tip may have originated. A guy who wouldn't mind throwing egg on our faces." In response to Lyons's querying look, he explained, "Vince Borrego. He rents from Mrs. Rios, too."

Dark red suffused the chief's face. "Borrego's mixed up with my son?"

Hale backpedaled. "It might be a coincidence. I can ask if Mrs. Rios has observed them together."

You didn't have to be psychic to read the thoughts of the man across the desk. He'd been unhappy about the ex-chief's return to town and dismayed at the publicity that surrounded Vince's involvement in the fatal shooting. Having his predecessor underfoot as a private investigator didn't sit well, either. This latest revelation must feel like the last straw.

However, Lyons never acted petty or vindictive. "Don't target Vince as the bigmouth unless someone else fingers him. I'm not on a witch hunt and, if the allegations are true, he's simply doing his civic duty. However, I don't consider him a reliable source, so please get your information about my son elsewhere."

"Understood."

Hale realized that he'd tacitly accepted the assignment. Well, the case had to be investigated and the chief had chosen him. On the plus side, if he dealt with it effectively, the chief's goodwill might come in handy. Say, whenever Hale got around to seeking a promotion. Testing was only part of the procedure.

He collected a few items from his desk and headed outside to his unmarked department-issue car, which came equipped with a computer and other high-tech equipment. Hungrier than ever, he set course for Alessandro's Deli.

The usual lunch crowd thronged the terrace. Inside, more diners jammed the tiny tables and lines formed at the self-service counters. Pastrami, meatballs, tomato sauce. Man, those Italians had a gift.

Hale was waiting when, from the rear, he glimpsed a blonde at the head of his line gesturing toward a display of pasta salad. The young male clerk dropped the serving spoon, apologized profusely and proceeded to stuff so much salad into a container that dribs and drabs spilled out as he forced it shut.

Typical foolish response to a pretty lady, Hale supposed. He might have reacted the same way at that age.

The clerk rang up the sale and the customer lifted her sack. When she turned, his heart did a silly skip-and-race kind of thing. Connie.

Hearts don't race. And grown men didn't feel a jolt of pleasure at glimpsing a woman they saw practically every day. Still, with the inviting part of her lips and that confident air, she had something special. One of these days he intended to read a book of poetry and find out what it was.

Hale felt a ping of disappointment when, dodging between tables to reach the exit, she passed without noticing him. Okay, so he had a bit in common with that gaping clerk. And with the three or four other guys whose heads swiveled to watch Connie. However, they hadn't spent yesterday replanting her flower bed while she bent over tantalizingly to inspect his work. The way she'd looked in shorts and a blouse had made him attack the soil with renewed vigor.

She vanished. When he got to his sandwich, he ate it in his car, then set out along curving Arches Avenue toward the central area of Villazon, where small apartment structures salted the mix of houses and duplexes. According to the information the chief had provided, Yolanda Rios lived on Lily Lane, a few blocks from the high school.

The only people Hale observed nearby were a couple of gardeners mowing and doing edging across the street. Before getting out of the car, he collected a few fliers concerning burglaries in the area, which he'd brought as an excuse in case he ran into Ben. The burglary suspect's description—young and thin, trendy clothes—indicated a possible high-school student.

Since most burglaries involved dopers, that raised the possibility their guy might be none other than Ben himself. One witness had mentioned a spider tattoo on the forearm, which the chief's son lacked, but a crafty crook might have applied a temporary one to confuse the description.

As Hale emerged, he noticed a flickering light through the curtains of the downstairs apartment on the left. Just as he put that together with the sharp scent in the air, a smoke alarm shrilled inside the building.

Fire!

First act: dial 911. As Hale conveyed the details, he remembered that the fire engines from the main station had rolled to the warehouse blaze. A delay of even a few minutes could spell the difference between life and death for occupants.

"I'm going to check if anyone's inside," he informed the dispatcher.

"Hang on." A beat later, she returned to the line. "The owner just called. We told her to vacate and that you're at the location. She doesn't believe anyone else is home."

"I'll bang on doors just in case." He'd better move fast, because a fire could rage out of control in minutes. Older structures provided plenty of fuel, including furniture that failed to meet current safety standards.

"Use caution, Detective," the dispatcher advised. "Can you stay on the line?"

"Sorry, no." Holding a phone would slow him. "I'll call when I'm done."

He was flipping the device shut when down the steps hurried Mrs. Rios, arms around a fuzzy dog, her graying hair mussed and her glasses askew. "Hale! I'm glad you happened by!"

"I have to make sure everyone's out," he informed her.

"Vince's at his office. Ben left for class half an hour ago. That's his apartment." She indicated the flames consuming the curtains. "I saw Paula go out a while ago." She stopped and gazed upward. "Oh, no!"

In the window directly above the burning unit appeared a boy's face. With a shock, Hale recognized Skip. "She left him alone?"

"I'm afraid so." Yolanda sounded as dismayed as he felt.

"Skip!" Hale yelled. "Come down!" If the boy moved fast, he could descend the stairs before the fire reached them.

The child didn't move.

The flames were going to climb the curtains and flash over the ceiling. Once they broke through the floor or mounted the hall staircase, they'd cut off escape. Wherever the firefighters had been sent from, Hale didn't even hear a siren yet. He couldn't wait for them to arrive.

Fear must have frozen the boy. "I'm going in," he told Yolanda. "Key?"

She handed him one. "This opens all the doors."

"Thanks." Taking a deep breath, he ran toward the entrance.

Chapter Three

The building had a straightforward layout, Hale discovered as he dashed into the main hallway: one unit on each side and stairs straight ahead. Eyes smarting and ears ringing from the smoke alarms, he raced to the second floor.

Fires spread fast. Before flames shot into the hall and blocked their escape, he had to reach Skip.

First he banged on Vince's door in case Yolanda had been mistaken, although it was hard to imagine anyone ignoring the noise. Then he unlocked the Laytons' apartment and, feeling no heat from the door and knob, entered.

In the living room, smoke seeped through vents and the heat from directly below made Hale sweat beneath his jacket. When he shouted the boy's name, an acrid lungful stirred a cough.

"Help!" The plaintive cry confirmed the boy's presence in a bedroom down the hall.

Hale ran in that direction. He stopped at the first door and went in. Obviously the master bedroom. No kid by the window.

Back in the hall, it was getting darker and hotter. Tougher to breathe, too. Hale darted into the next room, a bathroom, where he grabbed a towel, soaked it and, holding it over his nose and mouth, lunged into the hallway again.

Entering the last room, he felt a draft. Open window, blocked by a screen. Skip was huddled on the floor, a little ball of terror. He sprang up when he saw Hale and flung himself at him.

Hale transferred the towel to the boy's face. "Hold this!" he commanded, and the boy obeyed.

Split-second decision: to retreat the way he'd come or risk a two-story drop. One of Hale's firefighter pals had said people frequently died heading for a door when they could easily have gone through a window. The awareness that the fire lay directly beneath their path, and the memory of the smoky staircase that by now must be ten times worse, simplified the choice.

"Stand here!" He positioned the child away from the window, against the wall. Balancing on one leg, Hale smashed his heel into the screen. The bloody thing held. Why did this always look so easy on television? Grumbling, he seized a chair and swung. The jolt as it hit the frame reverberated through his elbows and shoulders, but mercifully, the screen went flying.

Skip remained in place. Calling a few words of encouragement, Hale seized the twin-size mattress and heaved it outside. When it landed, Yolanda directed a couple of male volunteers to position it as a landing cushion. The woman exuded a natural air of authority.

Hale crouched by Skip. In the light from the window, the boy's freckles stood out in a face white with fear. *Keep steady and calm, and he'll follow suit.*

"Here's what we're going to do," Hale explained. "I'll lower you outside as far as I can, then let you fall. Mrs. Rios is there. You'll land on the mattress, okay?"

"Okay." Skip clutched the towel.

"You'll be fine." Kids were supposed to be resilient.

Trusting blue eyes met his dark ones. "You'll jump, too, right?"

"Absolutely." For a fraction of a second, he felt as if he were staring into the depths of the kid's soul. Glimpsing a whole, complicated person whose future depended utterly on him. "Ready?"

The youngster straightened. "Yeah."

More and more of a struggle to suck in air, let alone talk. "Sit on the sill." Hale assisted the boy into place, facing outward. "I'm going to ease you down."

The child tensed almost to the point of rigidity. The mattress must seem far below, but if he didn't relax, he'd be more likely to suffer injury.

"Pretend this is a game. This is a playground and you're playing superhero, okay? You can do it!"

"Yeah. Okay, Hale." He sounded shaky but determined.

From far off, Hale heard a siren, but the crackle of flames was much closer and the smoke reeked of whatever combustibles were feeding the blaze. They didn't dare delay.

The boy's weight pulled Hale forward and, with his hands occupied, he had to brace his thighs against the sill. "One, two, three." A slow stretch as far as he could, and then, as he let go, he shouted, "Bombs away!"

An unexpected noise floated to him. Skip's laughter.

Below, the boy hit the mattress and tumbled forward. His hands skidded off the padding onto the grass but he appeared to be unhurt. Yolanda scooped the child into her arms, fussing over him while clearing the area for Hale's jump.

More sirens. Another minute, maybe, and they'd be here. Except Hale couldn't hold his breath that long, and his skin was about to peel off.

Hey, this ought to be no big deal. He kept fit in the workout room at the PD and swam regularly at home. He'd pulled his share of daredevil stunts over the years, too, including skydiving.

Piece of coke. No, wait, that's cake. Okay, so he couldn't think straight. And he had to do this facing the building instead of face-forward in order to lower himself as far as possible. He hung there feeling gravity suck the blood out of his arms, reminded himself that if he died the department would give him a fancy funeral, and dropped.

Almost missed the mattress. Tried to bend his knees to break the fall, lost his balance and toppled over. Mercifully, his head hit the padding, but pain shot through his left ankle and the side of his body throbbed.

Now he was supposed to rise, dust himself off and demonstrate to Skip how a he-man handled danger. With aplomb. With panache.

Fierce heat radiated from the nearest window that at any moment might explode outward. And Hale couldn't move, not even to drag his aching body out of danger.

"Somebody get me outta here!" he shouted.

A fire truck screamed to a halt on the street, boots pounded across the lawn and someone lowered a stretcher. *About time you clowns showed up,* Hale meant to say, but his larynx refused to cooperate.

He focused on suppressing a groan as his rescuers braced him for removal. Their precautions emphasized that he might have broken something important.

For the first time, the reality of the risk he'd run occurred to Hale. But he and Skip had both survived, and that was what counted.

* * *

Connie loved soap in its many shapes, colors and scents, prettily packaged, whether alone or in combination with bottles of perfume and lotion. Not only did soap make great gifts, but customers who bought it for their own use generally returned regularly for replacements.

"I shouldn't spare the time but I'm desperate! Can't you smell the smoke on me?" inquired one of her regulars, reporter-editor Tracy Johnson, who stopped in about four o'clock for a box of her favorite rosettes. Without waiting for an answer, she said, "I'm on deadline, and I'll be writing my fool head off this evening, but I refuse to scrub with the powdered stuff we use at the office. It feels like sandpaper and smells like shoe polish."

A hard-driving woman in her thirties, Tracy had few vanities. She wore practical pantsuits, tied her auburn-streaked brown hair in a ponytail and chose flat shoes over heels despite her small stature. She stopped in to Connie's Curios mostly for the candy bars but had developed a fondness for rose-scented soap.

The reference to smoke reminded Connie of the sirens she'd heard intermittently during the afternoon. On the radio, she'd caught a mention of a warehouse blaze. "Did anyone get hurt?"

"Depends on which fire you mean." Tracy chose a bottle of cucumber lotion. "I could use this, too. My hands are so dry they're cracking."

"There was more than one?"

"Two at once, can you believe that? I had to bring Roy in to help. He's okay if I tell him who to talk to and what to ask, but he never digs beneath the surface." The fiftysomething Roy Anderson mostly sold ads and handled layout.

"Where was the biggest fire?" Connie asked in concern.

"In a warehouse south of the Amber View housing tract." Tracy explained that a tenant had failed to obtain permits for storing chemicals used at an off-site manufacturing plant. A substance that spilled during unloading had ignited, thanks to a carelessly discarded cigarette. Without information about the exact nature of the chemicals, the fire department had had to assume the worst. Extinguishing a potentially toxic blaze required the hazardous materials team and, of course, added to the danger for firefighters.

"Somebody's going to pay a big fine and maybe go to jail," Tracy concluded. "Fortunately, nobody got hurt, but the factory owner violated a bunch of laws."

"People don't recognize the purpose behind safety regulations until there's a crisis, I suppose." Connie had been astounded by the red tape necessary to open a shop. She still wasn't convinced it had all been necessary.

"The second fire's a more interesting case," Tracy added. "The cause hasn't been determined, for one thing."

Connie glanced over as Paris Larouche, Jo Anne's twenty-year-old daughter, arrived for her shift. While ringing up Tracy's purchases, she inquired, "Where was the other fire?"

"At a fourplex that belongs to Yolanda Rios," the reporter answered. "You must know her from tutoring."

Yolanda's fourplex, where Skip lived? A wave of fear sucked the moisture from Connie's throat. "Was anyone injured?"

Unaware of the urgency behind the question, Tracy said vaguely, "Some idiot left a kid home alone but a cop rescued him."

She must mean Skip, since he was the only child in the building. "Is the boy okay?"

"A few scratches. He's been turned over

to Child Protective Services." The reporter signed her credit slip. "I guess Detective Crandall merits another commendation."

"Hale Crandall?" Connie asked, puzzled. "Why?"

"He got the kid out of the building."

Connie was grateful to the man once again. This must be a record. "Is he all right?"

"I'm not sure. The paramedics carted him off to the med center," Tracy responded. "The public information officer thinks he'll be okay, but that could be simply an assumption."

Anxiety swept through Connie. "Did you check on his condition?" *Tell me he suffered nothing worse than a little smoke inhalation.*

"The hospital refuses to comment." Tracy must have noticed her agitation, because she added, "Is he a friend of yours? I get so caught up in reporting that I can be insensitive."

"He's my neighbor." That seemed the simplest reply.

"He was awake and alert, if that means anything."

"Thanks." Paramedics often took people to the hospital as a precaution, Connie reflected, and summoned enough presence of mind to wish her visitor good luck with the articles.

After Tracy left, Connie discovered she was trembling. Once Saturday evening's incident with the intruder had passed, she'd never considered that Hale might get hurt somewhere else! Now he lay in the hospital, perhaps badly burned, and he didn't have relatives in the area. She hoped his colleagues were watching out for him. Or maybe he had a girlfriend, the Saturday-night date for whom he'd donned a suit and tie. Well, if that woman didn't rise to the occasion and take care of her man, Connie owed him a little TLC for saving Skip's life.

Thinking of Skip reminded her of Paula's poor judgment in leaving the boy unattended, and now he'd been turned over to social workers. Too bad Paris wasn't experienced enough to trust with locking up the shop, because if Connie could figure out where he was, she'd try to arrange custody now.

Seeking the most efficient way to ensure the boy's safety, she dialed Brian Phillips, the lawyer who'd helped with the adoption attempt. After she filled him in, he promised to track the boy. "I've got a few contacts at the county."

"That would be wonderful." How distressing that Skip might have to spend the night among strangers! As for how close she'd come to losing him altogether, she couldn't bear to think of it.

A year and a half ago, when he'd arrived at the tutoring center, he'd acted alternately clingy and rebellious. Connie's upbringing with divorced, self-absorbed parents—her mother was only slightly warmer than her father—hadn't prepared her to offer selfless nurturing. In fact, during her marriage, she'd resisted the notion of having children.

But with Yolanda's aid, she'd learned to be a steady, loving guide. While Skip was in kindergarten, Connie had helped him focus on classroom activities, following directions and acquiring a familiarity with numbers and letters. Later, they'd moved into reading and arithmetic. This month, he'd finished first grade working at or above average in all areas.

Now, without her, he might get lost in the system. She *had* to find him.

Well, Brian was working on that now, and sternly, Connie reminded herself that she had a job to do. After turning the counter over to Paris, she went into the office and settled at the computer to update her website. Mostly it informed customers of special events, but direct sales of custom items and collectables had been increasing steadily.

At six o'clock, she reversed the sign on the door to read Closed. As she collected her purse, her young sales assistant twisted a strand of light-brown hair around one finger and said, "I've been meaning to mention that I have a few weeks off later this month before summer school starts. I'd like to put in more hours, if it's okay."

Connie performed a quick mental calculation. Rearranging and freshening the merchandise at each of the three venues ought to boost sales enough to cover the extra wages. "That would be fine, if you don't mind rotating among the stores."

"Great!" Paris beamed. "I'll give you the exact dates tomorrow."

"I'll draw up a schedule with Marta and Rosa." Her managers would appreciate the extra help.

As the two of them exited by the front door and walked to their cars parked around the side, Connie thought about Hale's protectiveness on Saturday, and of the fact that he lay in the hospital after saving Skip. For heaven's sake, she'd never sleep tonight for worrying about his condition. Might as well drop by the med center. If the nurses were restricting visitors, they ought to at least allow a delivery from the gift shop.

It was closed now, but the concessionaire had privileges.

Hale had heard a variety of opinions about the Mesa View Medical Center. Captain Ferguson, grateful that cell phones and pagers had silenced the old public address calls for doctors, had declared it an oasis of calm following his hemorrhoid surgery. Sgt. Derek Reed, the PD's leading babe magnet, claimed the nurses got friendlier every year, but another officer had contended they were too preoccupied with paperwork to pay attention to patients.

Hale reluctantly agreed. His ankle throbbed—a sprain, the physician had said—and one side of his body had suffered massive bruises. Instead of offering sympathy and coddling, the nurse had instructed him to press a button on his intravenous line if he needed more pain relief.

Effective and modern, but not very warm.

The presence of fire investigator Andie

O'Reilly, who'd been debriefing him for the past half hour, provided a change, although she wasn't exactly the nurturing type, either. And in his opinion—which he kept to himself—fire officials shouldn't have flame-red hair.

Andie had arrived at the scene while the firefighters were tackling the blaze. She'd spoken briefly to Hale until the paramedics removed him, then begun interviewing Yolanda.

Her boss was supervising the chemical spill probe, Andie had explained, which left her to spend the afternoon locating and questioning the building's tenants before catching up with Hale again. Once the fire scene cooled and the building proved structurally safe, she'd comb it for clues.

Most fires began with cooking equipment, but to Hale it appeared this one had started in the living room. Although the place must be a charred, sodden mess, analyzing the burn pattern and sifting through the debris could, he knew, reveal amazing details.

"You're sure you didn't observe anyone when you arrived other than Mrs. Rios and Skip Enright?" Andie asked as Hale sipped a cup of tea to settle his smoke-irritated stomach.

"Only those gardeners across the way, as I

mentioned, and a few passersby who helped Yolanda," he said. "Why?"

She didn't answer. Since Andie had posed that particular inquiry twice before, there must be a reason.

"Hey, I was frank with you," Hale pointed out. In answer to a query, he'd confided the real reason for his visit, to which she'd replied that Chief Lyons had already informed her about the tip regarding Ben. That upped his respect for the chief, who seemed to be bending over backward to avoid the appearance of a cover-up. "Did you talk to Ben?"

"He denies any involvement with drugs. I didn't tell him about the rumor, by the way," Andie added. "Based on his history, I considered it a logical line of inquiry."

"So what's this about someone else at the scene?" Hale pressed.

She appeared to be weighing the advantages and disadvantages of disclosure. Possibly since he'd already provided his statement and therefore wasn't likely to be influenced, openness won.

"Mrs. Rios saw a man exit the building about twenty minutes before the fire started. Only glimpsed him from the rear." She consulted her notes. "Male, wearing a dark suit, stocky build, about six feet tall with brown hair. Might have been a salesman, although nobody knocked on her door."

"It wasn't Vince Borrego?"

"Mrs. Rios described our guy as taller and heavier. Also, Mr. Borrego was at his office with a client." Although there'd been a few earlier break-ins in the area, that suspect's description didn't match, either.

She switched off the tape recorder and shut her notebook. "Good thing you showed up there, Hale. Thanks to you, the kid's fine."

"Joel told me." Also that Skip had been removed from Paula's custody. And a darn good thing.

Hale hoped the DA brought child endangerment charges against the woman, who, according to Joel—on duty as watch commander—had gone out to buy baby clothes for her new grandchild. The fact that she'd been distraught about the situation softened his anger only marginally.

Rising, Andie brushed a wave of auburn hair behind one ear. The gesture might have struck him as flirtatious if not for Andie's no-nonsense manner. "Sure you're okay?" She cast a dubious glance at the untouched plate on his tray.

"I'd love a Twinkie," Hale hinted, not at all subtly. "Sugar usually settles my stomach."

"Sorry. I'm fresh out."

A tap at the entryway announced the arrival of a large floral display with slim, stocking-clad legs. He couldn't discern much of the newcomer's face. But he'd have recognized his neighbor's shapely limbs anywhere.

"Wow!" the investigator said. "That's a fantastic arrangement. Who sent it?"

"Courtesy of the gift shop," Connie announced from behind the flora. "These were the leftovers that wouldn't keep another day. And you are—?"

"Andrea O'Reilly. Fire department."

"Oh. You're investigating." The floral extravaganza navigated to a window ledge that already held several bouquets. "I'm Connie Simmons." Returning, she thrust out a hand, which Andie shook.

His new guest appeared to believe that introduction sufficed to explain who she was. And so it did. "Ah," Andie said. "You're Joel's ex."

"Precisely." Connie folded her arms, an action that emphasized the curves beneath her suit. It was startling to Hale how readily he responded even in his semidebilitated state.

"I guess dreams do come true, Detective," Andie remarked.

Was his reaction that obvious? Hale tugged the scanty covers higher over the hospital gown. "Yeah?" Luckily, before he said anything awkward, he realized she referred to a small bag that dangled from Connie's wrist. Imprinted with the legend Sandie's Tea Shoppe, it yielded an aroma so sweet and appetizing it penetrated the lingering scent of smoke in his nasal passages.

"Dessert?" Hale croaked.

"I doubted the hospital came up to your culinary standards. For junk food, anyway." She grimaced at the plate he'd been ignoring. "What on earth is that?"

"A liquid diet." Bouillon and flavored gelatin, neither of which he'd touched. "Do I smell baked goods?" Astonishing how rapidly his appetite returned.

"Enjoy your treat, folks." With a wave, Andie sauntered out.

Connie waited a couple of beats, then asked, "That *was* about the fire, correct?"

She sounded jealous. Unbelievable, yet gratifying, too. "She put me on the rack. I'm dying for sustenance."

"I'm glad you're not dying for real," she admitted.

"Really? You were worried?"

"That was brave of you." From the bag, Connie removed an array of the little snack cakes for which Sandie's had won local fame. "I couldn't bear it if something happened to Skip."

"The little guy behaved like a trooper." When Hale attempted to reach for a pastry, his body throbbed like crazy. Sinking against the pillow, he pressed a button to increase his dose of painkiller and waited for the misery to pass.

The bed dipped as Connie eased onto the mattress. When a soft hand stroked his temple, he felt like purring.

Man, what was wrong with him? Hale wondered. Another minute and he'd let her feed those pastries directly into his mouth. Must be the effect of the medication.

"Taste this. It'll distract you." She pressed a small portion of cake to his lips.

Vanilla. Too good to spit out. And never mind the crumbs. He suddenly decided he liked crumbs in bed. Tonight, he'd be happy to roll in crumbs. "Fantastic."

"Try some more." Another taste of heaven.

If the guys saw him like this, he'd be the laughingstock of the force. So what? Connie'd been worried. She'd brought him food. Which meant that maybe she found him as attractive as *he* found *her*.

It occurred to Hale that when he got home, he ought to act on the chemistry between him and his neighbor. Surely there was a statute of limitations after which a buddy's ex-wife became available to a guy.

But right now, he felt too good to worry about that.

Chapter Four

Shortly before 11:00 a.m. on Tuesday, Connie left Jo Anne and a part-timer at the shop to go retrieve Hale, who was scheduled to be released. She didn't usually run errands for him, but he'd earned this one.

Besides, if someone from the police station ran him home, details would get overlooked, such as whether he had the proper medical supplies or enough frozen dinners to last the next few days. Guys neglected things like that.

At the medical center, she dropped in to the gift shop. Marta Lawson, Connie's cousin and the concession manager, greeted her warmly.

"The new puzzles are selling like crazy."

Small and vibrant, Marta indicated a display of colorful devices from Japan. They were her personal find from an internet source. "Folks in the lobby love playing while they wait. Watching them sit for hours during surgeries makes me appreciate even more what you and Rachel went through for me."

A decade earlier, an automobile accident had nearly claimed Marta's life as she and Connie were driving to classes at California State University, Fullerton. Rachel, a police science student with whom they'd attended high school, had rushed from the curb and rescued her just before the vehicle burst into flames. Badly injured, Marta had spent years in rehab and still bore scars. Connie's broken arm had quickly healed.

Since Marta's mother had died several years earlier, Connie and Rachel had spent many hours sitting by her bedside and, later, escorting her to therapy. In the process, the three had bonded tightly.

"You'd do the same for either of us," Connie pointed out. "In fact, if you hadn't invited me to the tutoring center, I'd never have met Skip." Despite her disabilities, Marta had helped Yolanda organize the center, known as Villa Corazon. A play on the name Villazon, it meant "Town of the Heart" in Spanish.

"Speaking of Skip, any word about him?" her cousin asked.

"I tried to reach my lawyer this morning, but the secretary said he'd gone out. I guess he's in court." Connie had also left several messages at protective services but so far had received no response.

Across the lobby, an elevator opened. A middle-aged woman in a volunteer's pink uniform emerged, pushing Hale in a wheelchair.

"Oh, my gosh!" Connie said. "He's worse off than I realized." Then she remembered. "Oh, yeah, hospitals always put patients in wheelchairs before releasing them. Why, do you suppose?"

"Something to do with liability if they trip on their way out, I think." Marta indicated the volunteer following them with a pair of crutches. "He *is* injured, though."

"Sprained ankle, he mentioned." Connie's gaze lingered on Hale. In a sport shirt and sculpted jeans, his frame seemed too powerful to be confined. Someone had brought him fresh clothes, Connie observed, and hoped it was Joel rather than that striking red-haired fire investigator.

"I wondered when you'd quit fighting it," Marta murmured.

"Quit fighting what?" Connie signaled to catch Hale's attention. He must have cracked a joke, because both volunteers were chuckling.

"You've been staring at that man like you're dying of thirst and he's an oasis." Her cousin shook her head. "Sorry, I don't mean to pry. But when you look at him, the air sizzles."

Connie didn't want Marta to misinterpret the tension between her and Hale. "Sure, he's sexy. I'd have to be blind not to notice. That doesn't make him my type."

Her cousin sighed. "At least you don't have to worry that you're not *his* type." She had an unrequited crush on Sgt. Derek Reed, who treated her like a kid sister. As the PD's new community liaison and information officer, Derek coordinated a public-service program with the hospital. According to Hale, he'd dated so many nurses that he'd earned the nickname Sergeant Hit and Run.

In any case, Connie had no illusions about how differently she and Hale viewed life. To him, leisure time was just one long excuse to party. "Definitely not my type," she repeated.

"Waiting for me?" the subject of the conversation remarked as his beaming aide wheeled him closer. "I didn't expect a fan club."

One of the volunteers addressed Connie. "Mrs. Crandall? Here are the instructions for icing his ankle." She produced a printed sheet along with a couple of pouches. "Those are cold packs. They don't require refrigeration."

"Thanks." Connie didn't correct the woman's mistake, although she could tell it amused Hale.

"I have to escort him all the way outside," the volunteer added.

Taking the hint, Connie accepted the crutches from the other volunteer and thanked her. "Great job with the puzzles, Marta," she said by way of farewell.

Her cousin smiled. "Good luck with Skip!"

"Thanks for reminding me." Connie checked her cell phone again in case she'd missed a message. Nothing.

Outside, Connie brought her car around. Hale made a show of struggling to rise from the chair and hobbling to the passenger side. Dropping an arm heavily around her shoulders, he announced, "I don't know what I'd do without you, honey."

Connie rolled her eyes.

"And don't forget to stay off the ankle for the next few days," the volunteer said.

"Yes, ma'am," he responded solemnly.

Connie stowed the crutches in back. When she got behind the wheel, she found his presence a bit unnerving. Too big. Too sprawling.

"Stay in your own space," she grumbled as his knee bumped hers.

"Sorry, honey," he drawled. "We invalids aren't in full control of our movements."

"You'd better take control or I'm dumping you on the nearest street corner!"

"Okay, okay. Just one favor." As they rolled toward the exit, he indicated the police station across the street. "Turn in there. I need to pick up some files."

"Excuse me?" Connie kept her gaze fixed on the red light.

"The department insists I take off the rest of the week, but there's plenty I can do from home," he said. "Park by the side entrance."

"The department insists on leave for a reason," Connie retorted. "I'm assuming they've assigned you to a counselor, right?" The PD contracted with a local psychologist to assist officers after stressful incidents. "This week, that's your job. If you intend to break the rules, find another enabler." She pulled onto Mesa View Boulevard and bypassed the station.

"Fine." Hale rapid-dialed his phone. She caught her ex-husband's name in the ensuing conversation, along with a description of the cases in question. "Satisfied?" he asked after he hung up.

Connie refused to comment further. "Do you have enough food at home?"

"Fully stocked." Apparently deciding to yank her chain, he elaborated, "At least three bags of chips plus a six-pack."

"Are we stopping for groceries? Last chance!" she declared as they approached a supermarket.

He moaned melodramatically. "We'd better go straight home. I'll have to rely on the charity of my beautiful neighbor to rescue me from famine."

He grinned broadly. The man was impossible. And outrageously charming.

Connie used the tactic she often employed when she failed to one-up the guy. She changed the subject. "When are you seeing the shrink?"

"Dr. Wrigley dropped by this morning." He winced as he shifted on the seat. "Her office is next door, so she strolled over. Guess she figured I'd duck her otherwise."

"Which you would have." Most cops of Connie's acquaintance fought their darndest against accepting help, particularly of the psychological variety. "How did it go?"

"She asked how I felt. I told her, 'Sore.' End of story." He waved away the matter.

She heard a catch in his voice. "No nightmares?"

He seemed to weigh whether to give an honest answer. Finally his mouth twisted wryly. "One or two. I've spent better nights." He didn't elaborate. "But it's par for the course."

One session with Dr. Wrigley hadn't been enough. "Did you set an appointment?"

"Yeah, I agreed to have my psyche massaged Thursday morning, but only to keep the department from ragging on me," he grumbled. "The sooner I put the incident behind me, the better."

As she parked in front of Hale's house, she remembered how fiercely he'd plunged after that softball on Saturday. A mere three days later, another plunge, this one far more extreme, and he could hardly walk. She was reminded again of her vow early in her marriage never to forget the fragility of life.

"I'll help you." Connie unlocked the doors and lifted the crutches from the rear seat.

"I can handle it." As Hale dragged himself from the car, he grunted unwillingly. "Maybe I should have accepted more painkillers."

"Did they give you a prescription? I'll fill it," Connie offered.

He dug into a pocket and provided the slip. "Didn't expect to be this achy."

She handed him the crutches. "I'd offer a shoulder but I doubt I could support you." At five foot three, she barely reached his chest.

"Nothing to it." Despite the bold words, he studied the walkway as if it stretched for miles. "Race you to the porch."

"Sure." Strolling alongside, Connie felt sympathetic twinges as her neighbor hobbled across the cement. He strained to negotiate the steps that he usually vaulted with ease.

When they entered, he stared around the living room at the pool table and motorcycle posters as if he'd been gone for ages. "Good to be home."

"Be it ever so humble," she added.

He proceeded into the family room and sank onto a couch facing the big-screen TV.

Remote at hand, he appeared unlikely to rise again for quite a while.

"I'll fix you lunch." Connie cast a dubious glance at the cabinets. "How about soup? And ibuprofen."

"You read a guy's mind." His attempt to sound jaunty fell short. "Are you in a hurry?"

She'd cleared her schedule until a two o'clock meeting with her bookkeeper. Finances were an unavoidable part of operating a business. "I can stay for a bit. Why?"

He gestured toward the ankle he'd elevated onto an ottoman. "Care to ice that like the lady suggested?"

Playing nurse suited Connie's nurturing instincts, especially to a helpless male who usually appeared so strong. Besides, left on his own, Hale might neglect his treatment. "Done, soldier. Soup first or later?"

"First, if it's quick." His lids drifted down sleepily.

When she brushed a lock of dark hair off his forehead, he released a sigh so unguarded that she nearly bent to brush a kiss across his cheek. The prospect of his teasing her for the action stopped her.

In the kitchen, Connie opened a can of soup. Since Hale appeared to be dozing, she rinsed a couple of dishes and stuck them into the nearly full dishwasher, which she loaded with the soap and switched on.

She returned a box of crackers to a shelf, stowed a jar of olives in the fridge and wiped the counter. Squelching the temptation to straighten the entire house, Connie located ibuprofen and heated the soup.

Why bother to impose order when he'd only restore the mess? Anyway, she'd never be satisfied until she'd thrown out the motley furnishings and redecorated.

Which would be going way overboard.

Hale awoke, swallowed the pills and ate the soup. Up close, she observed the signatures festooning his pressure bandage. The names belonged to nurses and a few fellow officers, including Derek and Joel. And Andie O'Reilly. That would be the fire investigator.

Well, she isn't the person cooking him lunch and tending his injury, is she? Connie derived a surprising amount of satisfaction from that thought.

She read the instructions for icing the ankle. The gel pack required squeezing and shaking to activate whatever scientific breakthrough created instant coldness. "It's single-use,"

Connie noted. "I'll pick up more when I fill your prescription."

"Got a bag of peas in the freezer?" Hale asked. "Those work just as well. And I can reuse them."

"You're kidding!" She'd never considered peas a medical treatment.

"I played basketball in high school. Coach taught us all the tricks."

"I'll bring some over later. It'll probably be your closest encounter with a vegetable in months." She positioned a chair alongside the ottoman.

"Ouch!"

Connie glared. "I haven't touched your ankle!"

"I meant the remark. I eat at least one salad a week."

She found the end of the bandage, which peeled off easily. "Once a week? Are you sure that isn't overdoing the health thing?"

"Hey. Sarcasm is *my* department, not yours." The crack lacked his usual zest. Apparently exhausted, he leaned back and surrendered to her care.

The directions advised performing an ice massage, a term that sounded too cozy for her taste, so she moved quickly to the specifics. "Apply ice or cold pack directly to injury. Move the ice frequently so it doesn't remain in one spot."

Wrapping her hand in a kitchen towel she'd brought for the purpose, Connie gently rubbed the packet against Hale's lower leg. Dark bruising continued beneath his jeans, she observed. The entire side of his body must be purple.

She had no difficulty envisioning the well-proportioned thighs and torso, flat stomach and broad chest, since Hale spent most weekends hanging out in cutoffs sans shirt. But she'd never seen him in distress, or stroked him like this, either. Never felt his pain easing beneath her hands and relaxation flowing through him.

Unlike her, Hale had a gift for living in the moment, evidently untroubled by recriminations from the past or worries about the future. Perhaps that helped explain his contradictory mixture of adolescence and adult male strength.

He appeared completely at peace right now. Luxuriating in her touch, lost in a sensuous daze. Or perhaps simply falling asleep.

His eyes opened. Definitely not asleep. Enlarged pupils—and she wasn't imagining the increased breathing rate. Instinctively Connie drew back, and realized her hand had grown chilled.

She set the pack aside. "If you'd like to carry on with this, be my guest."

He studied her lazily. "Nothing could compare to your touch, angel."

Upset at being treated like an object of seduction, she snapped, "That's a good line. You should use it on a susceptible female."

"Which you're not?" Hale asked sweetly.

Connie felt heat rise to her cheeks, and to cover it grabbed a roll of pressure bandage and began winding it around his foot and calf. Snug without cutting off circulation, as the flier advised. "Don't call me *angel.* Or sweetheart or honeybunch, or any of your other smarmy endearments!"

"Smarmy?" he echoed.

"Naive women must melt when you shower them with phony compliments. Well, not me!" She smacked the end of the bandage so it clung without requiring an adhesive.

He flinched. Connie felt guilty, but not enough to apologize.

"Okay, okay." Hale shrugged. "I have a naturally flirtatious manner. Don't take it personally."

"Exactly my point!" Too late, she realized that her remark might be misinterpreted as meaning she *wanted* him to get personal. The sooner she scrammed, the better. "I'm due at the store. My bookkeeper'll be there in twenty minutes."

"Don't forget dinner," he mumbled.

"Order pizza!" Miffed, although unsure exactly why, she rose and grabbed her purse. "I'll drop off the frozen peas in a minute."

"Leave the door unlocked. I don't think I can move."

The quavering tone nearly softened her mood until she recognized that he was playing on her sympathies. "Suit yourself."

Out she went. Irked at Hale, as always, until the sight of two figures on her porch drove him completely out of her awareness.

Despite the stomp of retreating footsteps, Hale basked in the residual glow of Connie's attentions. Okay, maybe the ibuprofen lightened his mood, too, but that woman had cast a spell on him.

Then she'd punctured it with one flick of a fingernail. Or, rather, one stab of her sharp tongue.

The blond halo and appealing softness

promised heaven, but let him so much as glance at her with a trace of hunger and what did he get? A fast brush-off.

The woman exerted a pernicious influence. Arriving with her, he'd experienced a flutter of embarrassment at the state of his rooms, which made no sense, since he would loathe living in a china dollhouse. One of these days he ought to redecorate in his father's style, with hunting rifles slung over the fireplace and shabby stuffed deer heads on the walls. Well, perhaps not.

From outside, the murmur of a conversation drifted in. Who was Connie talking to?

A man's voice reached him, and then a high-pitched one, like a child's. Hale's skin prickled as he caught his own name.

He wished they'd speak louder. When Connie responded, he discerned only, "Hospital… much better…" Then the traffic noise from a block away eased and the words came clear.

"I was scared," piped the youngster.

"You've been incredibly brave," Connie replied.

"I was scared for Hale," the child explained.

The image of a small figure huddled beneath a window. The boy's shape in his arms…heavy smoke…the scream of an alarm…

Shaking off the flashback, Hale strained to rise. Blessing Connie for positioning the crutches within reach, he lurched to his feet.

Thanks to the ice and pills, the throb along his left side had dulled. Eager to greet the boy, Hale made his way to the door. En route, he had to bat a stray tennis shoe out of his path with a crutch and nearly slipped on a magazine he'd thrown wide of the wastebasket the other night. He ought to either hire a maid or improve his aim.

He hobbled onto the porch. On the walkway next door, Connie threw her arms around a tall, football-player-type guy. Grumpily, Hale decided that the fellow possessed nothing he himself couldn't match, with a cool pair of crutches thrown in for good measure.

Then a skinny munchkin pelted through the replanted flower bed and clumped across the grass, shedding soil with every step, to fling himself at Hale. "You're okay! You're okay!"

Skip's last sight of him had been as the paramedics hauled Hale away on a stretcher, a fact that hadn't registered until now. Judging by the boy's comments, he'd been fretting ever since.

"A bit banged up but whole. I'm glad *you* weren't hurt." Reaching clumsily over one crutch, he ruffled the boy's hair. "What're you doing here, champ?"

"Mr. Phillips brought me." He indicated the Viking, who in Hale's opinion took way too long to separate from Connie. "He's a 'turney."

An attorney. That explained the hug—simple gratitude, he presumed. "Sprung you from the lockup, eh?"

"Yeah!" The kid's blue eyes shone. "He says I can stay with Connie!"

Satisfaction swelled inside Hale. He hadn't realized how much he'd grown to like the boy. "That's great news." They'd survived a crisis together, and now they were neighbors.

An idea dawned. Far from his usual sort of escapade, it involved neither beer nor barbecuing and probably wouldn't amuse his buddies, either. Still, he *had* resolved to breach Connie's castle ramparts, hadn't he?

"We'll do stuff together," he promised. "Once this leg heals, we can use my pool. Know how to swim?"

A headshake. "Can you teach me?"

"You bet." He'd lay odds that Connie would insist on watching or even participating. That meant she'd arrive in her bikini, a spectator event that in Hale's book ranked a close second to the Super Bowl.

The Viking slid into his expensive car. Connie waved before crossing to Hale. "Isn't this fantastic? Thanks to Brian, I'm getting custody of Skip! Of course, adoption takes time, but since I've already completed the home study, Brian says—"

Hale had heard more than enough about Brian. "I'm pleased for you. Skip and I are already making plans."

"What sort of plans?"

The boy beamed at his new mother. "Hale's going to teach me to swim!"

Startled pause. Bosom heaving with indignation. Better not stare or he'd ruin everything. "When I'm better, of course," Hale amended. "Ought to pool-safe your son."

"I won't allow him anywhere near that pool until you buy a cover with a child alarm," she retorted. "And I'm locking the gate between our properties." During her marriage Hale and her ex had installed a gate in the wall so Joel could sneak over for a beer while supposedly gardening. Since then, Hale, who occasionally pitched in to prune a bush or patch a hose, had persuaded Connie to leave her yard accessible.

Under the circumstances, however, a lock seemed wise. As for the cover, Hale had always considered the wall around his rear yard a sufficient safety measure, but the possibility of fishing a limp Skip from the pool sent shudders through him.

"Send me a bill for the lock. I'm the one who owns the hazard," he responded. "And I'll look into covers as soon as I'm better."

Connie's jaw shut. Argument circumvented.

Pursuing the advantage, Hale said, "You go meet your bookkeeper. Skip can play at my house 'til you finish."

"But I have to stay at the store until six." Her gaze strayed to the newly arrived suitcase on her porch. "And you can barely walk."

"A six-year-old doesn't require a nursemaid," Hale pressed. "Only a responsible adult on the premises. Which may not fit your usual opinion of me, but I did save him once, you'll recall."

Connie blew out a long breath. "I should call Keri Sommers. She operates a home day care."

"I'm sure he'll love it there—tomorrow.

Don't forget he's already spent one night with strangers. Can't hurt to stick close to home today." Hale tapped his watch. "Time's a-wasting. I won't let him anywhere near the water. Promise to stay inside, okay?" he said, addressing Skip. "And never, ever, go near the pool without an adult."

"Okay!" He hopped about joyfully. "Wow! I get to play at Hale's!"

The boy's enthusiasm did the trick. "Let me fetch his suitcase. And those frozen peas." Connie returned with record speed, also bringing a box of granola bars for a snack. "You have milk, I presume?"

"What do you think I pour over my cereal?" Discretion prevented Hale from admitting that he'd doused his cornflakes with orange juice once or twice when he'd neglected to shop. "I'll read to him, too."

"You own children's books?" Strong skepticism.

He conceded he didn't. "I'll locate something appropriate on the computer." Thinking fast, he added, "To which I plan to attach a child filter as soon as possible."

"You're being awfully cooperative," Connie complained. "If I weren't in such a rush..."

"Trust me," Hale said. "Oh, and Connie?"

"Yes?"

"Don't forget to bring home dinner for the three of us."

For a second, he feared he'd pushed her too far. Then her nose wrinkled, a sign of reluctant assent. "You win this round. And, Hale, thanks. But I suspect you're going to earn that dinner."

"No problem." Grinning at the little boy, Hale mused that he'd finally won a round with his cantankerous neighbor.

Chapter Five

Babysitting when his body screamed to collapse and never move again wasn't the best idea Hale ever had. Luckily, Skip's energy waned after an hour or so of reading newspaper comics, playing videogames and surfing child-friendly sites on the computer in the home office.

Hale put the boy to bed on an inflatable mattress in the laughably titled guest room amid unused exercise equipment, old computer parts, an outdated game system that he couldn't part with for sentimental reasons and boxes of sporting gear. The kid was asleep in seconds.

Which is pretty much what happened to Hale when he lay on his bed for a few minutes of shut-eye. He slept restlessly, skimming the surface of a confused dream. Connie stood behind the store counter, pointing to a shadow in the rear room…had to chase him…crutches refused to function…falling, falling…

A shriek pierced the dream. Hale awoke fast, realized who must be screaming and grabbed the crutches. He launched himself across the room and into the hall despite the barbed assault of a thousand nerve endings.

"What's wrong?" Bursting into the guest room, he half expected to find the boy grappling with an intruder or buried beneath a pile of fallen gear.

Instead, Skip thrashed on the mattress, his comforter bunched at one side. His eyes were shut.

"Hey, Skip." Gently, he nudged the dreamer with a sock-clad toe, since his muscles refused to consider bending. "You're having a nightmare."

Glassy eyes opened. At last they focused. "Huh?"

"Why'd you yell?" he asked.

The boy squirmed into a sitting position. "I had to run. From the fire."

"Wasn't I there?"

"I couldn't find you." Freckles stood out against his pale face.

"I'd have saved you!" For extra measure, Hale noted, "Since you're living with Connie, I'll be right next door."

A smile bloomed in response. "I'm glad."

"Me, too." The statement seemed inadequate to reassure the kid that most houses didn't burst into flames. Still, the little guy appeared content for the moment. "Hungry?"

Skip scrambled to his feet. "Yeah."

"A pretty lady left us granola bars." Hale hobbled into the kitchen behind his guest.

Until today, he hadn't given any thought to the probability that children, like adults, could suffer from posttraumatic stress. Heck, the kid had not only faced death, he'd lost his family, and not for the first time. According to Connie, the boy had been removed from his birth family because of drug abuse and neglect.

As they ate, Hale tried to decide how best to bolster the boy's confidence. The worst part of his own dream had been the sense of helplessness. That had vanished on waking, perhaps because, as a policeman, he had real-world training and experience in handling danger.

Skip could use a dose of the same, in child-tailored proportions. "You've gone through some scary stuff," Hale began.

A wide gaze met his above the rim of a glass. "I guess so."

"People can't always protect themselves," he said. "But I can teach you to stay safe most of the time. Interested?"

A dubious nod.

"Most danger is preventable," Hale went on. "You're more powerful than you think."

"Yeah?" The boy grew perkier.

"Let's start in the kitchen." Dragging ideas from musty corners of his brain, Hale reminded Skip of how quickly the fire had spread in the apartment. "Never play with matches and don't cook without a grown-up. Don't cut things with a knife, either, unless someone helps you. People often land in the emergency room from cutting themselves accidentally."

"I don't cook," Skip informed him. "I just microwave."

"Popcorn?"

"Yeah!"

"Ever burn it?"

"Once." A wry expression. "I burned my fingers, too."

"Exactly. 'Til you're older, make sure an adult is around first, okay? If you're hungry, just ask Connie or your babysitter for help."

Skip frowned. "What about you?"

"I'll be here. One door over." Hale didn't mean to assume the role of father figure, but a big brother—now, that idea appealed. "We're not finished vanquishing danger. Let's talk about seat belts."

The little guy's face twisted. "They're boring."

Hale recited statistics, simplified for his audience, about how seat belts saved lives.

"Can I ride in your car?" Skip asked.

"When my ankle gets better, absolutely. *With* your belt on." To keep the boy's interest from flagging, he moved to the computer. As they played with it, he told Skip, "When you're older, you might chat with people online. Never tell anybody your name or phone number or where you live. Bad guys may pretend to be your friend, or lie and say they're children, but you can outsmart them."

"They won't trick me!" Skip's chin lifted.

Seeing the buoyancy return, Hale decided

to quit while he was ahead. So he agreed to let the boy play a G-rated videogame.

Hale hadn't expected to enjoy their interaction so much. Kids in general still didn't interest him, but he got a kick out of observing what made this particular one tick.

A throb reminded him to ice his ankle. Leaving Skip in the office, he removed the bag of peas from the freezer and carted it to the living room.

Through the window, he spotted Joel Simmons striding along the sidewalk. In slacks and a sport shirt, the guy had a classic look: light-brown hair, clean-cut jawline, regular features. Too bad about the eyebrows. In the two years since his divorce, they'd descended into a more or less perpetual frown.

Joel ought to find a girlfriend. He'd be a lot happier and Hale wouldn't experience twinges of guilt for lusting after Connie.

His friend rapped twice and, without waiting, opened the door. "Yo," he said to Hale. "How's the cripple… I mean, hero?"

"Sore." He set aside the bag of peas and eyed a sack bearing the logo of the humorously named Pickle Ice Cream Shoppe. "A gift? For me?"

"I nearly bought you an all-expenses-paid

trip to Las Vegas with a couple of showgirls thrown in, but I figured you'd prefer this."

Joel fetched a scoop, spoons and bowls from the kitchen while Hale assessed the two cartons. The flavors were chocolate with fudge chips, and vanilla with cherries and sweet pickle chunks. That last one sounded bizarre, even to him.

"New flavor?" he asked.

"Yup. It was today's special." Joel perched on a folding chair.

Hale decided to postpone alerting his small visitor to the treat so he and Joel could talk. "What about the files I requested?"

"The lieutenant's reviewing them for possible reassignment." That made sense, but irked Hale anyway. "You hear they caught the burglar?"

"No kidding!" Although it wasn't his case, Hale took a particular interest because the description had suggested Ben. "Who is it?"

"Fifteen-year-old high school student named Stuart Yothers. A woman saw him opening her neighbor's sliding glass door. We recovered electronic gear from the other break-ins at his house."

That put the chief's son in the clear. "His parents didn't notice the stuff?"

"He'd stashed it in his bedroom." Between bites of ice cream, Joel continued. "Here's the interesting part. Stuart claims to have known that Ben Lyons never locked his apartment because one of his friends hangs out there. Our underage perp says he'd have burglarized the place except he figured anybody who ripped off the chief's son would get hunted down."

"Why is it so interesting that Ben didn't lock his door?" Foolish, maybe. And perhaps an indication of innocence, since a dealer almost certainly *would* secure the place to protect his drugs and cash.

"An unlocked door means anyone had access. Add that to the fact that Mrs. Rios saw a stranger on the premises," Joe said. He rocked back in the chair. "Andie's tight-lipped about her findings. She and Vinson—" that would be fire chief Neil Vinson "—spent an hour closeted with the chief this afternoon."

Hale finished his scoop of chocolate and started on the vanilla. A tangy bite of pickle went smoothly with the other flavors. "Good stuff."

"Yeah. I might buy this flavor again. But not soon."

A rustling from the hallway preceded Skip's eager cry of "Ice cream!"

Joel regarded the newcomer as if a hobbit had popped out of a hole in the floor. "Who're you?"

The boy paused. "Skip. Who're you?"

"This is Joel. He's a cop, too." To his friend, Hale explained, "Skip's the little guy who rescued me from the fire."

Skip giggled. "*You* rescued *me!*"

Joel took his cue from Hale. "I heard you were a brave young man. Guess you saved each other. Care for a bowl, sport?"

"You bet!"

With Hale's permission, Skip took his ice cream to the computer room. "I suppose I'm teaching him bad habits," Hale said. "Connie probably doesn't allow eating outside the kitchen."

"What's Connie got to do with him?" As usual at the mention of his ex-wife, Joel bristled.

Hale hadn't intended to drag her into the conversation, but how could he avoid it? "She's planning to adopt Skip. I'm just watching him today."

Joel's eyebrows knitted into a fierce line. "She's suddenly interested in motherhood?"

Okay, Crandall, shut up now. But with Joel regarding him expectantly, he finished, "She says she bonded with him at Villa Corazon."

Joel smacked his dish onto a TV tray. "That's great. Just great." He lurched to his feet and began to pace. "When I suggested having a baby, she couldn't be bothered. Too busy becoming Villazon's newest entrepreneur."

"You wanted kids?" That was news to Hale. Joel had reacted to the pressure of testifying with an almost manic desire to party and hadn't eased off much since.

"I'm from a big family. Of course I expect to be a dad." Joel pounded his fist on the mantel. Good thing it didn't hold breakable gewgaws like at Connie's house. During the turbulent days before their separation, the guy must have wreaked havoc. "So I'm stuck paying alimony for another three years to support the family she finally decided to have. Is that unfair or what?"

"And she got the house, too," Hale added sympathetically, before realizing that he'd added fuel to the fire. Anyway, Connie had taken out a loan to repay her ex-husband's share, he recalled. "Alimony sucks. But you *did* lose half her inheritance."

"That Web business sounded like a sure thing." Joel had impulsively followed a tip from a fellow cop about a start-up company that turned out to be fraudulent.

"You did kind of abuse her trust." She'd deposited the money in a joint bank account even though, under California community property law, the inheritance belonged to her alone.

Joel's anger gathered momentum. "So what? That doesn't excuse *her* disloyalty. She acted as if testifying against a fellow officer and the chief was no big deal. *My duty,* she called it. I'm still catching flak over that whole scene."

"You are?" Hale hadn't heard any rumblings in the department recently. He began rewrapping his ankle.

Joel responded with an irritated gesture. "Dropped by Jose's Tavern on Friday and guess who I ran into?" Off-duty officers patronized the tavern, which offered a big-screen TV and a free buffet of nachos, Mexican meatballs, chips and salsa on weekends. "Norm Kinsey."

At last report, the disgraced former lieutenant had been employed as a security guard for a nephew's business in Montana. "What's he doing in town?"

"Visiting relatives, I gathered from one of the other guys. Norm and I didn't exactly indulge in a cozy chat." Joel glared at an invisible enemy. "I sat down with my beer, nowhere near him, and flirted a little with the waitress. Out of the blue, he started making snide remarks about me to his buddies, extra loud for my benefit."

A veteran nearing sixty, Norm had been bitter about losing his pension, and the man's pals obviously sympathized. Most of them had left the department since the scandal, but whenever Hale saw one of them around town, he got an uneasy sensation. After all, he'd also testified.

"You let it go, right?" he asked.

"As long as humanly possible. I'd have decked him if he weren't such an old duffer. Skin looks gray and I recalled he had a heart condition. So I told him to take his sorry butt home to Montana, and left."

Hale stuck down the end of the bandage. He'd fixed it neatly, although not as well as Connie. "Well, thanks for the ice cream, buddy. I'll check into those files ASAP."

"When are you due at the bureau? Monday?" The question drifted to him as his guest carried half-empty cartons to the freezer.

"I'm visiting Dr. Wrigley Thursday morning. I'll drop by afterward."

"Suit yourself." Joel ambled back. "Can you drive yet?"

"Sure. It's my left ankle that's hurt. And I'm fine as long as I avoid prescription meds."

"If you're short a ride, call me." Joel opened the door. And froze. "Well, what a less than thrilling surprise." Next door, an engine died. Perfect—or rather, rotten—timing. Another minute and the former married couple would have missed each other. "Nice car she drives. New?"

"Fairly." The maroon sedan, which its owner proudly washed and waxed each week, had arrived six months ago. Joel still drove the battered blue pickup he'd owned since before the marriage.

Connie couldn't have missed the truck, or the sight of her ex standing in the entrance. Hale wished she'd leave Skip here and go inside 'til her ex drove off, but timidity wasn't her style. Nor Joel's.

Through the window, he observed her progress toward them. "How about not starting World War Three in my house?"

"We just have a few little matters to discuss," came the less-than-reassuring reply.

Hale pointed toward the hallway door. "At least shut that." If these two launched into a row, he preferred to shield Skip.

"Sure." Joel complied. While he was doing so, his ex-wife swung inside. She toted an Alessandro's shopping bag redolent of lasagna.

Hale had to admire Connie's boldness. Although she stood eight inches shorter than her ex, she matched him in orneriness. Amazing that they'd both survived their combustible marriage.

"I don't want trouble with you," she told Joel. "I brought Hale's prescription and his dinner."

"You won't forget to feed that cute little boy you're adopting, I hope," her former spouse returned with deceptive calm.

"Leave him out of it."

"Okay." He chose another sore topic. "Your new car is impressive. Boutiques must be big moneymakers."

"It's leased." Connie stalked to the kitchen. Hale heard the clunk of her purchases hitting the counter. "Stop it, Joel."

The blockhead followed. Unwilling to risk leaving them alone, Hale pried his aching body upright and hobbled in their wake.

As host, his job included the prevention of bloodshed.

"Easier if we discuss this person-to-person without lawyers, I figure," Joel was saying. "Two years of payments seem enough to me. Especially when you can afford those snazzy wheels, not to mention an addition to the family. With three stores, anybody can see you're rolling in money."

"Most of my profits go into upgrading the stock and hiring additional staff," she retorted across the counter. "My savings account is rock bottom, I have no pension and I didn't get a share of yours, either. You're lucky you only have three more years of payments. You'll still be far short of repaying my grandparents' money."

Joel's face flushed with rage. "*You're* lucky I've been so reasonable about the whole bloody situation! Lost my house, lost the family I should have had, and now you act like you're doing me a favor. I'd be careful where I parked that car, if I were you."

To Hale, the remark seemed like empty bluster to save face. Nevertheless, he loathed bullying in any form.

"Is that a threat?" Connie demanded furiously.

"I hope it isn't, because like it or not, you made me a witness," Hale reminded his buddy.

Joel glared. What did the guy expect? He *had* issued a threat.

The man returned his attention to his ex. "If you'll review your priorities," he growled, "you'll realize that messing with me isn't one of them." On that ugly note, he strode out.

After the door slammed, Connie drew a shaky breath. "That jerk!"

While Hale doubted his friend would resort to vandalism, he obviously held a grudge. "It might be worth sacrificing the alimony to shut his yap."

She wheeled on him. "I should have known you'd agree with your friend!"

"I don't." Hale hadn't mastered the art of maneuvering on crutches well enough to retreat. Standing only inches from her irate form, he replied mildly, "I simply offered a suggestion. And I'm as much your friend as his."

Connie surprised him by throwing her arms around him. She smelled of flowers and femininity.

"What's this for?" Despite the crutches, he managed to hug her in return.

"Thanks for saying you'd be a witness and that you're my friend. I need somebody in my corner." Connie nestled close to the curve of his throat.

Was he in her corner? Hale felt guilty for abandoning his old buddy. And guiltier for the things he'd like to do with his old buddy's former spouse.

If he didn't disengage, he'd regret it. On the other hand, a guy afraid to take risks might as well be dead. So Hale did something he'd been longing to for years.

He kissed her.

Chapter Six

For Connie, instinct took over. Boldly, she met Hale's tongue with hers, relishing the moan that tore from deep in his throat and the eagerness with which he angled against her. Oh, how she'd ached to be touched, and, she discovered to her astonishment, by no one else but him.

One minute she'd been poised for an argument and now her skin tingled as they came together. The pressure of his mouth and the slight roughness of his cheek beneath her palm awoke a dangerous hunger. To feel his hard chest against her breasts. To open herself to him and let longing carry them both on a wild, uncharted path.

To make the same mistakes as when she'd fallen for her husband.

But Hale wasn't Joel, and she didn't have to go any further than she chose. Why not relish this freedom, this excitement? The sofa beckoned, a haven from crutches and gravity.

Dimly, she recalled that they weren't alone in the house. And that, distracted by her ex, she hadn't checked on Skip since her arrival.

The flush of passion receded as reality intruded. She wriggled out of Hale's embrace. "Stop."

When his attempt to reach for her ended in a wince, he protested, "What's your hurry?"

"For a whole lot of reasons, this is a bad idea." She moved to put the counter between them. "I'll dish out your share of the lasagna."

"No reason we can't eat together." Spoken in a hurt-puppy manner.

"I promised you dinner. I never promised you company." She dug through the drawers for a spatula. "By the way, I've arranged for Skip to attend Keri's home day care from now on. Thanks for taking care of him today. How'd he do?"

"He's a great kid." Hale watched through

heavy-lidded eyes. With his hair mussed, he looked as if he'd been rousted out of bed.

Perversely, Connie wondered what sleeping with him would be like. *Only once, to get him out of my system.* Yes, sure. As if anyone with half a brain would believe that!

"I'm usually home on weekends," he added. "I'll be glad to pitch in if you need me."

Lasagna sauce slopped onto Connie's fingers as a lopsided slice defied her attempt at precision. Irked, she finished cutting the piece and then rinsed her hand.

"That won't be necessary." She'd decided to hire more help to free her Saturdays and Sundays, despite the expense. "I'm sure we'll be fine."

"Skip enjoys the contact with me," Hale persisted. "I think we're good for each other, because we're both guys and because of what we experienced at the fire scene. He and I—"

"Were strangers until a couple of days ago. Whereas I've spent a year and a half with him." Connie tore off a chunk of garlic bread and dropped it on the plate beside the noodles. "I appreciate the kindness, but you aren't Skip's new dad. You're the guy next door."

"And I'd better not forget it?"

"Don't cast me as the bad guy. Changing

families is a huge adjustment for Skip. I intend to avoid further confusion about who his parent is and where he belongs." She set out the plate with a napkin, fork and knife, and filled a glass with ice and water from the fridge. "How's your leg?"

He hesitated before admitting, "It hurts like crazy."

She indicated the pharmacy vial. "Take one of those."

"I'd love to." Hale sank onto a stool at the counter. "But they contain narcotics, which can linger in your system overnight. That would make it illegal for me to drive tomorrow."

"Why do you have to drive tomorrow?"

"I don't. But I might choose to."

If he neglected his health, Connie supposed that wasn't her concern. "Do as you please. Meanwhile, I'll collect my son." Intellectually, she supposed she might be rushing matters to use that term, but regarded it as an open declaration of her commitment.

"He's down the hall in my office. Let me reimburse you for the food and the meds." He glanced around for his wallet.

"Only if you let me pay you for watching Skip," she insisted.

He grumbled a negative response. Connie's bad mood receded. Really, he'd been kind, and perhaps Skip *could* use masculine companionship. Eager to see her son, she hurried along the hall to the office. Skip was perched at a desk facing a computer. Before he registered her presence, she stood drinking in the sight of her little boy. The realization that this child had been entrusted to her care filled Connie with tenderness.

Skip gave her a quick glance. "Hi."

"Hi, sweetie." She skirted the edge of the desk. "Ready to go home?"

His gaze clung to the screen. "I'm kinda busy."

"Aren't you hungry?" she asked. "I brought lasagna and garlic bread."

"Later, okay?"

She circled behind and saw that he was manipulating a squat cartoon figure darting through a forest. Blam! An attacker hit the ground. Boom! A shot whizzed by the character's head.

She couldn't blame Hale for letting the kid play, considering that his injuries prevented his supervising the boy outdoors. And Yolanda had taught her that children often had trouble making the transition from one activity to another, which explained Skip's stubbornness.

So she waited until the scene ended. "Now," she said firmly. "We have to go home."

"Where?" He dragged his attention from the computer.

"You live with me now, remember?" Sympathetically, she noted, "Staying with me may seem strange at first, but we're a family. We'll have fun, and you can always count on me."

Paying no attention to her little speech, Skip darted past. She found him in the kitchen, sitting on a stool as Hale finished his meal.

"I'll stay here," the boy said.

A choking noise issued from Hale. "Sorry, guy."

"I like this place!" He folded his arms.

"Honey, we have to leave," Connie said.

"No! Go away!"

She'd expected a certain amount of acting out, or at least she'd been prepared in theory. In reality, his rejection stung. Connie wished she knew how to respond to such open defiance.

She disliked hearing parents plead with kids, and bribery set the wrong tone entirely. Pulling rank, however, would antagonize the boy. Locked in an ongoing battle of wills, particularly at this stage, he might even run away.

She considered herself Skip's mother, but he obviously didn't. Not yet. Unsure how to proceed and beginning to question her preparation for the major job she'd undertaken, she searched for the right words.

Hale leaped into the gap. "Let's set a few ground rules," he told the child. "Number one, the grown-ups are in charge around here, not you."

Skip chewed his lip.

"Number two, you live at Connie's house. You can visit me when she and I say so. And I'll only say so if you're polite to your mom. Got that?"

A reluctant nod. The boy's acquiescence stirred relief, yet Connie couldn't help wondering why *she* didn't possess whatever intuition Hale was drawing upon.

He continued addressing the boy. "Now I'll talk to you like a young man instead of a baby, all right?"

Skip nodded uncertainly. Connie held her peace, fascinated by the unfamiliar sight of her neighbor behaving maturely.

"We'd all like to have fun every minute, but that's not possible. Connie's taken on a big job. She's willing to help you grow up," he informed the child. "When you're mean to her or do bad stuff, you hurt her, and that's not right. You have to respect your mother."

Skip turned woeful eyes to Connie. "I'm sorry," he said.

"I love you," she replied, her throat squeezing.

If she hadn't already thrown her arms around Hale once this evening, she'd have done it again. He'd sensed exactly how to reach the boy, and he'd done so without undercutting her.

If the past was any indication, Hale could be expected to commit an irresponsible act very soon. But for the moment, he'd earned a get-out-of-a-tongue-lashing-free card.

"Thank you, Hale." Connie meant that from the heart. "Well, Skip, can we go now? I'm starving."

He hopped off the stool. "Is there any ice cream left? The kind with pickles?"

She assumed he was joking, until Hale said, "You're welcome to it."

Skip ran to the freezer, stood on tiptoe and claimed a carton. As he headed out, Hale called, "Hold the door for your mom!"

Amazingly, the boy obeyed.

Connie sought to convey how impressed she was. And discovered she'd never developed a vocabulary for complimenting Hale.

"You did great," she blurted, and followed her son outside.

He walked carefully along the sidewalk instead of dashing through the flower bed, and wiped his feet on the mat while she unlocked her house. "You're quite a gentleman," Connie told him.

"Yeah. Like a grown-up," he answered solemnly.

Although she doubted this angelic behavior would last long, Connie felt as if they'd cleared the first hurdle on their path. And she owed this success to Hale.

The boy had lapped up the masculine attention. While she didn't exactly concede the point about his requiring a father figure, keeping Hale involved might be a good thing, as long as he respected her boundaries.

In a mellow mood, Connie helped Skip set the table. Then they sat down to their first meal as mother and son.

Optimism must have fuzzed Hale's brain when he'd assumed he'd be driving on Wednesday, or that he'd feel well enough to investigate cases by phone. Instead, pain drove him to swallow pills that night and the next morning, with the result that he spent the day floating several inches above the furniture.

Connie phoned to ask about bringing supper. When he learned that she'd have to drop off the food because her friends Rachel and Russ McKenzie had invited her and Skip for dinner, he declined.

Although pleased that Skip had hit it off with five-year-old Lauren McKenzie at Keri's that day, he missed his little friend. And the air didn't smell right without a hint of Connie's perfume.

Still, a couple of his pals, patrolman Bill Norton and Sergeant Mark Rohan, supplied him with the bare necessities: chips, salsa and an action DVD. As they were leaving, Derek Reed arrived with a supply of tacos and a rented videogame.

As the new community liaison, Derek worked a regular nine-to-five shift. Hale thought the chief would have assigned such a visible post to a politically ambitious soul, but for some reason he'd named Derek, who'd acted disgruntled ever since.

The two men settled in the den and snuffed a few rounds of alien invaders while munching. Stray bits of lettuce and taco shell spilled around them.

"Do dogs eat this junk?" Hale asked as he surveyed the mess on the sofa and carpet. "Getting a pooch might be easier than cleaning."

"You think dogs are easy?" Derek replied. "Gotta walk 'em, take 'em to the vet, feed 'em and scoop the poop."

Skip might enjoy a dog. On the other hand, dogs did tend to destroy flower beds, Hale recalled. "Forget I mentioned it. I'll figure out who borrowed my vacuum one of these days."

"I did. I'll drop it off." Derek propped his shoes on the scuffed coffee table. "Don't suppose any of the guys told you the latest about your fire."

They hadn't, since the patrol and traffic divisions lacked an inside track to investigations. As public liaison, Derek's dealings with the press required him to keep current if only to determine which questions to dodge.

"What's going on?"

"The fire originated in Ben's living room couch. Likely source is a cigarette," Derek explained.

Careless but not criminal. "The chief must be happy about that."

"Guess I forgot the part where it was marijuana." His companion pressed the controller to blast another battalion of space freaks.

"Yeah, you left that out." Though smoking pot fell short of dealing drugs, it didn't bode well for a convicted drug user. "They find anything else?"

"Another roach in a wastebasket. No cash or drug paraphernalia, though."

"So the kid's busted." A judge would probably revoke his parole.

"Looks that way." Derek fired off another round.

Hale had lost interest in computerized villains. An unexpected emotion twisted inside him: disappointment. The few occasions he'd met Ben, he'd liked the kid. Then a possibility occurred to him. "Ben reportedly let friends hang out there. Any chance one of them was at fault?"

"Hard to tell. They couldn't lift any prints or DNA off the roaches."

"That's interesting." If the smoker had held the roaches with a clip, that explained the lack of prints, but one would still expect a trace of saliva. "What about that man Mrs. Rios saw leaving the building?"

"Unaccounted for. Ben claims he's been framed. He couldn't provide a name or a motive, though." He added sarcastically, "I can't imagine who might resent the department that much, can you?"

Motive and opportunity pointed toward Vince. Too many loose ends to be certain, though. Yolanda's mystery man, for instance, and Vince's alibi. Also, a guy didn't usually torch his own place just to spite someone else. He hoped Andie had searched Borrego's apartment, either with a warrant or with his permission, for signs of marijuana, incendiary devices or a suspicious absence of valuables that would indicate he'd anticipated the fire.

"Have the newspapers picked up on the marijuana angle?" Hale asked.

"Not yet, but that Johnson woman asks a lot of questions," Derek groused. "I'm betting she'll ferret it out."

"That ought to tick off the chief," he observed.

"She'll have to stand in line. He's angry at a lot of people, not least of whom is his son." The sergeant switched off the game and started channel surfing.

"So much for father-son rapport." Hale wondered how those two had gotten so far off track. If he had a son, he'd place communication and mutual respect above anything else. Except his wife, of course.

Still, unlike Will Lyons, he hadn't lost the woman he loved to cancer. Maybe grief had prevented the chief from recognizing his son's problems until too late.

Hale settled back to watch a raunchy sitcom. By the time Derek left, he felt so sleepy he turned in, but dozed only intermittently, awakening repeatedly in the midst of disturbing dreams.

On Thursday morning, he awoke feeling drained and achy. Although tempted to cancel the appointment with Dr. Wrigley to catch up on his shut-eye, Hale knew he'd better find out what was bothering him.

Hale drove through the residential streets slowly, aware of an unaccustomed shakiness and wondering if it was a side effect of pain medication. Since he'd taken his last pill the previous afternoon, he doubted it.

Encountering a red light at Villa Avenue, he stopped, then watched for a traffic break to make a right turn. When a stretch opened, his nerve failed. Despite a more than adequate margin for error, he waited for a green light.

What was wrong with him? He'd never lost his nerve like that before.

Abruptly, Hale hit the brake. Tires squealed, the car threatened to fishtail and he narrowly stayed in his lane. Why hadn't he noticed the car changing lanes ahead of him? Then he crept below the speed limit to Mesa View Boulevard, ignoring the impatient honking from the car behind.

The doctors' building lay on the left. Hale idled until the oncoming lane stretched empty for a block, then turned and rolled into a handicapped slot, since a doctor had arranged for him to receive a temporary placard.

Dr. Wrigley's office occupied a corner of the second floor. She kept an efficient schedule, and the secretary summoned Hale quickly. A good thing he hadn't canceled the meeting. Best to deal with this attack of nerves before it got out of hand.

He balanced on the crutches while shaking hands with Eugenia Wrigley. A tall woman in her fifties with gray-streaked hair and a straightforward manner, she'd become the department's psychologist ten years ago, and had met with officers regularly during the scandals. Being married to a retired firefighter gave her special insight. None of which changed Hale's basic opinion that shrinks were for wackos.

"How's it going?" She remained standing while he chose the love seat. Then she settled into a chair.

Hale's father would have told him to keep this short and sweet. In Mack Crandall's day—he'd retired from the Villazon force ten years ago—officers had viewed psychologists with skepticism. Heck, they still did. By opening his yap, Hale risked being put on indefinite leave.

"I'm a little jumpy," he ventured.

"Tell me about it."

Eugenia listened as he described the bad dreams and the fearfulness while driving. Was he experiencing flashbacks? she asked. Anger? Depression?

"Bad dreams. A few brief flashbacks." He drew an uneasy breath. "What do you think?"

"Sounds like a normal response to acute stress," she answered.

Acute stress, huh? "All I did was jump out a window." Not a major trauma in the scheme of things. "What's the big deal?"

"How about the possibility of dying?"

"Me?" He'd been worried about Skip, not himself.

"Young men tend to think they're Teflon, and public safety officers are the worst examples," the psychologist explained. "At some point, we all have to confront our own mortality. Maybe at some level that's what hit you."

Smoke billowing around him. The hiss of flames. Striking the ground hard and pitching forward. It did make sense that his mind would replay the events whenever he lowered his guard.

"How long before I stop annoying the other motorists with my imitation of a little old lady?" He paused. "I guess what I really mean is, when can I go back to work?"

"When you feel comfortable doing so." Smoothly, Dr. Wrigley continued, "At the hospital, you described the fire scene like an observer. Just the facts, devoid of emotion. I'd like you to walk me through it again, without shielding your reactions."

How unpleasant, Hale thought. Still, it appeared necessary.

Baring his soul, he discovered, produced an effect similar to physical exertion. Although reliving the experience was a strain, in the end he felt better. Cleansed, somehow.

"I guess the fire affected me more than I realized," Hale admitted.

"First time you've been hurt in the line of duty?"

"Other than bruises, yes." He stretched. Pain a little milder, but still present and accounted for.

They talked more at length. Hale answered the doc's questions honestly and openly, and tried out her techniques for focusing on the here and now. To his surprise, he enjoyed it.

Before he left, Dr. Wrigley said "Drop in again if you continue to suffer effects."

"That's it?" he asked, startled. "I've had my tune-up and I'm cleared for action?"

"You're due at the department on Monday?" Reading confirmation in his face, she said, "As long as your mood stays positive and you don't experience further problems, you'll be fine. Otherwise, call me."

"I'll do that." Then Hale had another thought. "Doc, what about the little boy?" He sketched the situation with Connie and Skip. "Can doctors work with a child that young?"

"Definitely. Especially with the change in his family situation, he should see someone." From the desk, Dr. Wrigley produced a business card bearing the name Mike Federov, Ph.D., with the title Clinical Child Psychologist and an address in the same building. "Mike's great with kids."

"He sounds perfect." Hale wondered whether

Connie would interpret such a suggestion as criticism. He'd have to broach the subject carefully.

Downstairs, despite some stiffness, he felt easier about driving. The matter of Dr. Federov hung in his mind. He'd rather not risk having Skip overhear a discussion at home, so he swung by the gift shop.

Hale put the odds of Connie's resenting his interference at about nine to one. He only hoped the profit motive would discourage her from breaking any china doodads over his head.

Chapter Seven

When the phone rang at the store, Connie gave a start and exchanged glances with Jo Anne Larouche. Perched inside the front window ledge, the senior clerk grimaced. "Your turn."

"Believe me, I'd rather my employees didn't have to deal with this jerk." Bracing, she lifted the handset. "Connie's Curios."

"Hi, dear. It's Yolanda. How's Skip?" The familiar voice soothed her nerves like an application of cucumber lotion.

Connie rounded her finger and thumb, signaling "Okay" to Jo Anne. Her assistant returned to replacing the June wedding display of champagne flutes, cake toppers and bell-shaped cupcake pans with Fourth of July mugs, caps and T-shirts.

Yesterday and this morning, the shop had received half a dozen prank calls. They'd begun with hang-ups, which might indicate wrong numbers, but proceeded to heavy breathing at the other end of the line.

If this continued, Connie planned to notify the police and request a trace, although she wasn't optimistic about the result. Soraya Bloom, who owned the nail salon next door, had received a series of obscene calls a year ago that, the authorities had discovered, emanated from an untraceable cloned cell.

"He seems to like his room," she told Yolanda. "We picked out a new comforter and sheets together. He's making friends at the day care center, too." She declined to mention the boy's frenzied opposition to bedtime, a struggle that last night had lasted nearly an hour. "How are *you* getting along?" The four-plex blaze had taken a toll both emotionally and financially on the owner.

As Connie listened to the widow's account of how her two grown sons had pitched in, she kept an eye on a woman browsing the markdown shelf in one corner. A new customer, the fortyish shopper had waved away an offer of help and scurried to a far corner. That might indicate shyness, embarrassment about a tight budget or an intent to shoplift.

"My place stinks of smoke, although mercifully this side of the building is still livable," her old friend said. "We can't start major repairs until the investigators and the insurance adjuster finish tromping in and out, though."

The customer placed a couple of items in a clear basket looped over her arm. Nothing furtive about her behavior and, given her attention to the sale merchandise, she might simply be intimidated by the upscale appearance of the boutique.

Not too intimidated to venture inside, luckily. Connie valued bargain hunters who helped move less-popular or dated items. With limited space, she couldn't afford to let goods collect dust.

She kept one ear attuned as Yolanda filled in details about the tenants. Ben was staying with a friend while Vince remained in his unit, which Yolanda had scheduled for carpet shampooing and repainting. Apparently the authorities hadn't yet decided how to handle the evidence linking Ben to possible drug use.

"Miss O'Reilly from the fire department

keeps dropping by at odd hours to question him." Yolanda clicked her tongue. "Vince is getting testy about it."

"I'm sure the evidence will lead in the right direction." Chimes announced a young mother pushing a baby carriage. To Yolanda: "Hang on a sec." To the mom: "May I help you?"

"Just picking out a birthday card."

"We received a new batch yesterday. Let me know if you can't find what you want." Connie returned to Yolanda. "Have you heard any more from Paula Layton?"

"She stopped by yesterday." A waspish note underscored Yolanda's mention of the foster mother. "She says her lawyer believes she can plead guilty to a misdemeanor and perform community service. I suppose that's more useful to society than putting her in jail."

"I hope she learned a lesson." Both customers approached the counter. "I have to go, Yolanda. I'll bring Skip to the center to see you soon." Connie planned to carry on their formal tutoring sessions once school resumed.

"Wonderful. Keep me posted!"

Connie rang up the birthday card and a box of stationery for the young mom, and the sale items for the other customer. In the process, she obtained their email addresses for the store's mailing list. Both had expressed a strong interest in being notified about sales.

Shortly after they left, Jo Anne announced, "Hunk alert!" She enjoyed keeping watch out the window for interesting passersby.

Connie chuckled. "Hey, Jo Anne, you're an old married lady."

"But not dead!" responded her assistant. "Anyway, one bad experience is no reason for you to swear off men."

"Who says I swore off men?"

"Honey, when guys wander in here with their tongues hanging out, you bristle like a porcupine," Jo Anne said. "Be nice to this one. He's cute and he's on crutches."

Oh, *that* hunk. "He isn't a love interest. He's my neighbor." And, according to Skip's chatter, ideal in every way. Last night, the boy had thrown a tantrum when she refused to invite the man over for a play session. She might have succumbed except that she'd already changed into a bathrobe.

"There's no rule against flirting with your neighbor," Jo Anne persisted.

"He's my ex's best friend." Nevertheless, Connie peered out the window between red-white-and-blue rosettes. The guy had somehow managed to develop a cocky swagger even while poling along on supports. If anything, the exertion showed off his well-developed upper body.

Since she didn't wish to watch him struggling with the door, she opened it for him.

"Great service," Hale commented as he entered.

"One of these days I'll be able to afford an automatic door for our handicapped guests. Hunk… I mean, Hale, this is Jo Anne." She blushed furiously at her slip of the tongue.

He whistled. "I'll take the compliment. Ma'am, it's a pleasure to meet you."

"Likewise." The beaming clerk shook hands.

"What can I do for you?" Connie asked him.

Hale advanced into the store cautiously as if merely looking at objects might cause them to tumble and shatter. "I, uh, wondered if you carry sleeping potions."

He had to be kidding. "Try a drugstore."

"I don't mean pills. Some kind of tea or scented candles for relaxation."

Hold on. What was he really doing here? "You don't drink tea, you drink beer," Connie said. "What's this about?"

He cleared his throat. Instead of answering, however, he lifted a palm-size stuffed zebra. "Say, this is cute."

Although Connie recognized evasion when she saw it, the sight of the man's big hand cradling the creature was endearing. "If you're interested, we offer a ten percent discount to police and fire officials."

"Okay. I was attempting in my clumsy way to work the conversation around to..." Hale glanced toward Jo Anne, who'd returned to the task of decorating the window. In a low voice, he continued, "I visited Dr. Wrigley today. Got a clean bill of health, by the way. She said the nightmares are a normal reaction to stress."

Connie had forgotten Hale's earlier mention of them. His easygoing manner made it hard to picture him as a trauma victim. "So you're okay?"

"First rate. How about Skip? He had a nightmare about the fire when he was staying with me."

"Now you tell me! Maybe that's why he creates such a fuss about going to bed."

From his pocket, Hale produced a business card. "Dr. Wrigley gave this to me. I figured if a police officer can benefit from therapy, so can a kid."

Connie glanced at the card. Mike Federov, child psychologist. "As a matter of fact, Russ McKenzie recommended him. They're old friends. I was planning to phone him today."

"Oh." His grin went flat.

Understanding dawned. "You expected me to object."

"I figured you'd bite my head off."

"That's ridiculous!"

"It's what you usually do."

Much as she'd like to deny the accusation, she couldn't. "I suppose so, and I'm sorry." That brought Connie to an awkward point she'd been meaning to raise. "The truth is, although I value your friendship with my son, I'm apprehensive, too. He's been pressuring me to invite you over and I'm afraid he might get too attached to you, see you as a parent figure. But you're not the parent. *I* am."

That hadn't been easy to admit. She braced for a sarcastic retort.

Hale leaned against the counter. "A funny thing happened on Tuesday. I don't have much experience with kids, but I enjoyed figuring out how to connect on his level. He's a great little guy. I wouldn't mind serving as his big brother."

No irony. No smart-aleck remark. And the term *brother* softened Connie's resistance. "A bedtime story from you might allay some of his anxieties."

"I'd be happy to read to him."

Behind her, the phone rang. She flinched.

"Kinda jumpy," Hale observed.

"We've had some crank calls. Hang-ups and heavy breathing." Resolutely, she reached for the phone. "Connie's Curios."

A pause. *Please let someone speak. A customer. Even a "sorry, wrong number."*

Instead, a raspy breath. And then, tinnily, a strain of music. The familiar Carpenters recording of "We've Only Just Begun," which had once been her favorite song. With an oath, Connie slammed down the handset.

"That was him?" Hale said. "You should have handed it to me. Talking to a police officer tends to discourage these creeps."

That hadn't occurred to her. "I'm so accustomed to dealing with problems on my own, it didn't enter my mind," she conceded. "If it happens again, I will."

"Maybe I should stick around."

"He doesn't call *that* often."

Jo Anne leaned in from the window ledge. "Did the jerk say anything?"

"No. He played music." Connie identified the song.

"'We've Only Just Begun.' The words could be taken as a threat," Hale remarked. "I hope he's not planning to escalate the harassment."

That was a scary thought. "I don't understand why people do this kind of thing."

"It's a power play," her neighbor speculated.

"I had a stalker when Phil was overseas." Jo Anne's husband, a former marine, had served in the Middle East. Injured in a traffic accident two days after his return home, he now drew disability pay and filled orders for his wife's sideline business selling cosmetics. "A guy from my auto shop. He'd drive by my house and watch me. I was seeking a restraining order when he landed in jail for assaulting another woman."

"A lot of wackos out there," Hale agreed. "Could be a customer, a deliveryman—simply a guy who's developed an unhealthy crush."

Connie didn't recall any likely candidates. "Hearing that particular song bothers me. It was the theme for my wedding."

"Oh, yeah, I remember." Hale had served as best man.

A nasty suspicion reared its head. "Joel," Connie said.

"Whoa! This isn't his style."

She swallowed hard. "You only *think* you know him. He's got anger issues. He used to get furious at me when we were married. Once he punched his hand through the wall, and another time he threw a vase."

Hale looked shocked. "At you?"

"At the fireplace," she conceded. "He's bigger and stronger, and believe me, it was scary."

Hale seemed to be searching for a middle ground. "He shouldn't have done that, obviously. But that was a long time ago."

Connie disagreed. "He threatened me right in front of you. The phone calls started the next day. Who else would play our wedding theme?"

"That's still a leap," Hale protested.

"Not to a woman," Jo Anne said. Connie nearly cheered.

Their visitor raised one hand. "Wait. Let's view this objectively, okay, ladies?"

"We're talking about your best friend,"

Connie reminded him. "How objective does that make you?"

"Bear with me." He plowed ahead. "Have you heard the caller's voice?"

"No."

"Been bothered at home?"

Also negative. Joel had her unlisted number—but then, perhaps he wasn't stupid enough to point the finger at himself that plainly.

"Seen him in the vicinity?" Hale persisted.

She shook her head.

"So this could be anyone," he concluded.

"The morning after he attempted to browbeat me into giving up my alimony? Hardly!" To her, the motive overrode all else. "He was ticked off about my adopting, too. But when he started browbeating me with the idea of having a baby, it was *after* our marriage began falling apart. Guess he thought a baby would solve things."

"The timing might be a coincidence," Jo Anne murmured. Then she added quickly, "Not that I'm taking Joel's side!"

"She's examining the facts," Hale opined.

His comment irritated Connie further. "If you were the person being hassled, you wouldn't be so smug about it!"

The half smile vanished. "Point taken.

Okay, let me contact Joel and ask him directly. He's hot-tempered, but I've never known him to be sneaky. If he's seeking revenge, he won't hide it."

That *did* sound accurate. "Okay," Connie agreed. "I'll give him that chance. Then he'd better lay off or I'm filing a report."

"Fair enough. Meanwhile, keep a log of the calls—times, duration, background noises, anything the person says," Hale advised. "Here in California, you have to receive ten annoyance calls in twenty-four hours at a business for it to constitute a violation. Only one call at a residence is sufficient."

"Which Joel obviously knows!" Connie growled. "And I can't block the calls, as he's perfectly aware, because I'll lose customers. If I agreed to give up alimony, that's the last I'd hear of this!"

Hale's hand closed over hers. "You're really upset."

"I'm furious!" Also shaken, much as she hated to acknowledge the fact. Until now, she'd never considered Joel dangerous. Heavy breathing and a few hang-ups might seem minor to Hale, but they could escalate. "And worried. I mean, the man's armed."

He frowned. "That's a requirement of his job."

"You're telling me no cop ever turned that gun on his ex-wife?"

His face tightened. "I don't believe...well, I'll talk to him and see how he responds. This afternoon, if possible. Then tonight, I'll hobble over to your place and read Skip a night-night story. When's his bedtime?"

Behind his back, Jo Anne raised one fist in triumph, as if luring her neighbor constituted a triumph. Connie ignored her.

"Eight o'clock. I'd be grateful for your help, on both counts."

With Hale's aid, she hoped to weather this transitional period with Skip. As anxious as she felt about Joel, her long-term concerns centered on her son, who hadn't yet showed signs of bonding with her. To him, she probably seemed just another in a long line of unreliable adults. More than anything, Connie dreaded the possibility that, despite her best efforts, the adoption might fail because Skip had become mistrustful of attachments.

She'd never expected to rely on her neighbor in such an important matter. She hoped he wouldn't get bored too soon with playing big brother.

"See you tonight." Hale ambled out of the store.

Jo Anne opened her mouth as if to add an admiring remark. Catching Connie's glare, however, she thought the better of it.

Outside, clusters of teenagers strolled past along Arches Avenue, an indication that classes at the high school had ended. Several girls whom Connie recognized as costume jewelry devotees cut across the lot toward the store. Taking a deep breath, she prepared to wait on them.

Whatever her other concerns, she had to set them aside. Right now, business came first.

Still mulling over what approach to employ with Joel, Hale went home and rewrapped his ankle. In the process, he tried to sort out the puzzling impressions from the encounter with Connie.

More than once, he'd found himself viewing events through her eyes. What a strange yet illuminating experience.

Take the phone calls. Obnoxious and disruptive, sure. But frightening? He hadn't considered annoyance calls in that light, especially since the store appeared such a friendly, busy place. Yet her reaction reminded him of Connie's vulnerability last Saturday night when they'd heard noises in the storage room. Women had good cause to be sensitive to threats.

As for Joel, in the decade that they'd been friends, Hale had watched the guy romping with his nieces and nephews, collecting toys for a needy family at Christmas and mentoring young officers whose overconfidence put their lives at risk. The notion of Joel attacking his ex-wife didn't track. Or, at least, so Hale would have believed before he heard Connie's story about Joel's violent episodes.

Even decent people sometimes snapped. Afterward, friends and relatives always expressed disbelief. Hale couldn't afford to be complacent.

Well, he'd deal with Joel later. Right now, his eyes were drifting shut, so he stretched out in an easy chair.

A loud ringing woke him. His watch indicated he'd been asleep for twenty minutes.

"Crandall," he mumbled into the phone.

"It's Derek." He was calling on official business, the community liaison explained. Somehow the press had learned about the presence of marijuana in Ben Lyons's apartment.

"When TV vans start showing up, we've got to take charge or they'll pester us to death,"

Derek told him. "We've scheduled a press conference at three o'clock in the library. Easier to deal with them en masse than to answer the same questions a hundred times." The community room served for such functions since the police department lacked a large enough space.

"And you're waking me from my nap why?" Hale grumped.

His friend didn't bother to apologize. "You know what reporters are like when there's any whiff of scandal, always emphasizing the worst. We can't change their nature, but we can offer them a positive angle."

Hale groaned. "You mean me?"

"You're the hero who spotted the flames, ran inside and saved a little boy. Wear a uniform, please. It looks better in photos."

"Okay." He had less than an hour to find the one he'd hung in a closet and get presentable.

"Oh, and Hale?" Derek said.

"Yeah?"

"Don't forget your crutches." He clicked off.

Chapter Eight

Facing camera flashes and the din of overlapping questions, Hale mused that he'd rather jump from another burning building than deal with TV crews and reporters. But the honor of the Villazon PD was on the line.

Derek and Andie had reviewed the fire investigation and answered questions extensively before introducing Hale. Finally the press stopped baying after the possibility of Ben's marijuana use. Patiently, Hale answered their questions.

What ran through your mind as you jumped?

"I hoped I'd land on my butt rather than my head. Instead, I split the difference and crunched my leg." Smiles greeted this sally. Although Will Lyons's forehead furrowed, Derek gave a slight nod of approval.

Did you expect to die?

"I couldn't think that far ahead."

Do you consider yourself a hero?

"Lots of folks do braver things. Cancer patients suffer through chemotherapy. Military widows go on raising their families. I'm one among many."

This reply seemed to please the chief. Hale thought he might be in the clear until Tracy Johnson called, "Why did you go to the Rios apartments in the first place, Detective?"

Leave it to the local shark to home in on that point. Luckily, Hale had a ready response. "I was pursuing information about a burglar in the neighborhood. I'm pleased to say that our officers have since apprehended a suspect."

"How come you haven't 'apprehended' Ben Lyons yet?" demanded a man with fancy blow-dried hair.

Just like that, the leeches had resumed their quest for blood. Hale relinquished the podium to Derek, who replied, "As we said, our investigation of that incident is ongoing."

"Let's get real," the reporter persisted.

"If the suspect wasn't the police chief's son, you'd have tossed him in jail by now, wouldn't you?"

Will stepped to the microphone. "First, there is no *suspect* until we establish that a crime's been committed. So far, we have a fire that may or may not be accidental. As to my son's possible marijuana use, that's a matter for the district attorney to decide."

The chief halted as a side door opened to admit a rangy young man, his brown hair straggling across the collar of a sweatshirt. Why was Ben Lyons sticking his nose in here? Hale wondered.

Derek moved toward the newcomer as if to shepherd him away, but Ben dodged past. Short of wrestling him to the ground, there was no stopping him.

Will yielded the podium rather than argue in front of the press. His son strode to it and addressed the crowd.

"I'm the guy you're attacking, so I'll speak for myself." The kid swallowed hard as cameras swung into action. "For your information and for my father's, I did *not* smoke dope. I've been tested and I'm clean. Somebody's trying to frame me."

A clamor arose. Among the questions:

"Who?" and "Do you mean former Chief Borrego?"

"Not Vince!" Ben protested. "He's my friend."

"Kind of a coincidence that he lives in the same fourplex, wouldn't you say?" Tracy asked.

"Whatever you're implying, you're wrong!"

"Who else would set you up?" demanded a male reporter.

"I have no idea." Amid a storm of queries, the young man stared around, disconcerted. Although Hale sympathized, the kid had brought this on himself.

"Did your father put you up to coming here and declaring your innocence?" someone shouted.

"He wants nothing to do with me!" Ben squared his underdeveloped shoulders.

"Is that because you're an embarrassment?" The provocation came from a sharp-featured woman standing beside a minicam operator.

Before the offended youngster could lash out, Will seized the mike. "My son's going through a turbulent period, but he's a good kid. He's not trained to deal with the media, and I'd appreciate a little discretion from all of you."

Tracy had the grace to look sympathetic, or so Hale interpreted her reaction. Others, however, launched a barrage of comments, the theme of which was, "You've got to be kidding!"

Ben stood frozen, too stubborn or too confused to stop feeding himself to the wolves. Any second, Hale feared he might break and run. Since one couldn't expect mercy from wolves, he assumed such an act would be seen as a sign of instability.

A perfect opportunity for the local hero to breach the gap. Or fall through it, as the case might be.

"Hey!" Hale gestured for silence. Amazingly, it descended long enough for him to declare, "I'm the guy who nearly died in the fire, remember? If I'm willing to suspend judgment about its cause, you guys should, too."

He signaled Ben with a jerk of the head. Looking grateful, the young man accompanied him from the room and out a side exit. Outside, sunlight sparkled on a scene of almost shocking normalcy as moms escorted tots into the library and visitors descended the steps across the way at city hall. Hale felt as if he and Ben had narrowly escape a firing squad.

"I blew it, didn't I?" Hands on hips, Ben bent over as if winded. "I couldn't stand by and let Dad blacken my name."

"That's not what happened." Hale rested on the crutches. "He's done his best to be fair."

"Fair? Like staging this witch hunt in front of the whole world?" the youth snarled

Hale half expected the chief or another member of the brass to join them, but apparently the press kept them occupied. Their absence gave him the freedom to handle this matter his own way. "Can I tell you something in confidence?"

Ben looked interested. "Sure."

"I went to your apartment that day because your dad sent me." Hale hoped he wasn't going to land in trouble with the chief over this. "A reporter had phoned with a rumor that you were dealing drugs."

"What?" The boy bristled.

"Your father couldn't ignore the tip, but he refused to sic the narcs on you," Hale continued. "He asked me to talk to Mrs. Rios quietly, to see whether she'd noticed anything. He loves you, man. He doesn't welcome this circus, believe me."

"If he's so concerned about my feelings, why'd he send Captain Ferguson to snoop? That was before he heard that drug rumor, I bet," Ben said tightly.

"That's how parents act. He was worried." A buzz of voices alerted Hale that the conference had ended. The press must be leaving through the main exit, which lay out of view around a corner of the building.

"He's never cared what I felt." Ben sniffed. "When I have a son, I'll do things differently."

"Like how?" The topic interested Hale, both for Ben's sake and, potentially, for Skip's.

"I'll listen to him, for one thing." The young man's bitterness indicated how keenly he felt the lack of attention. "Respect his ideas and opinions. And if he makes a mistake, I won't push him away."

"Being a dad can get complicated, I guess." Beyond that, Hale had nothing insightful to offer, other than, "I recommend you lie low until this investigation plays out. Believe me, publicity won't improve your situation."

"I suppose not." With a final "Catch you later," Ben strode toward an aging sedan.

Hale noticed the chief, heading toward the police station with Derek, and saw the way he observed his son's movements with a mixture of regret and frustration. The guy clearly didn't know how to connect with him or heal their rift. Years earlier, connecting with his son might have been relatively simple, but there'd obviously been too many missteps to permit an easy reconciliation now.

Speaking of rifts, Hale sighted Joel unlocking his pickup. Shouting "Yo!" to halt his friend, he made his way between rows of parked vehicles.

As he did so, he cast a glance at patrolwoman Elise Masterson, a stunning blonde who loathed being treated like a girl. She, too, must have just ended her day shift. Wearing a black leather jacket despite the June heat, she pulled on a helmet, flung one jean-clad leg over her motorcycle and roared from the lot. On duty, she sometimes worked under Joel's supervision. Off duty, even though he'd testified in her harassment case against Vince, she ignored Joel's existence, along with virtually every other male in the PD.

"Why the blazes did Ben show up?" Joel asked when Hale reached him.

"To proclaim his innocence."

"I'm sure the vultures loved that!" His friend's annoyed gaze raked over a TV crew stashing equipment in a van.

"Are you referring to the distinguished ladies and gentlemen of the press? Jackals, maybe, but please don't insult our feathered friends the vultures."

Hale searched for a way to slip Connie's problem into the conversation. He was still debating when Joel asked, "Wanna grab a beer?"

"Sure. That'll go great with my painkillers," Hale joked, although in reality he hadn't taken any today.

"Meet you at Jose's."

"Give me fifteen minutes. Gotta change into civvies." He'd brought slacks and a shirt in the car.

They rendezvoused a quarter of an hour later at the nearly empty tavern, where they had no problem scoring a booth. The female bartender, a large-boned woman with a hearty manner, brought the beers herself. "Short on waitresses," she explained. "Good thing we're not busy."

"What happened to that cute blonde? What's her name—Laura?" Joel asked.

"She quit." The bartender distributed extra napkins. "We get a lot of turnover. Bet she'll be sorry she missed you." She strolled off.

"Was she flirting with me?" Joel asked Hale when the woman was out of earshot.

"Get over yourself!"

"Just curious."

After discussing the press conference, they lapsed into what would have been a comfortable silence had Hale not been carrying a burden. Finally, he figured out a nonaccusatory angle. "I'd better give you a heads-up."

"On what?" Joel stretched his shoulders. Sitting at the watch commander's desk gave a fellow cramped muscles and a sore butt, he often complained.

"Your ex." Hale described the annoyance calls. "When the creep played the theme song from your wedding, Connie got the idea it might be you."

"Typical," Joel muttered.

"He phoned a little after noon today," Hale noted. "If you were at your desk, we can establish your alibi."

A scowl. "I grabbed a sandwich at the deli."

Too bad. "The calls started the day after your argument."

"What argument?" Not receiving the sort of humorous response he'd apparently anticipated, Joel pinged his fingernail against the mug. "Hey, come on, Hale. Why're you bringing this to me?"

So much for ducking the issue. "I promised to mention it. Give you a chance to clear the air."

"Did you actually hear the call?" Joel pressed.

"Not exactly."

"I thought not! Sounds like the kind of thing she'd invent to shut me up," his friend responded. "An accusation like this could hurt my career, as she's well aware. I wonder how she expects me to pay alimony if I'm fired."

His friend was paranoid and truly ticked. Also mistaken, at least on one point. "That last call upset her pretty badly. I was there. She isn't faking." Hale recalled another point. "Also, an employee answered some of them. They're real, all right, and, under the circumstances, you have to admit her suspicion is logical."

Joel released an exasperated sigh. "Okay, so some loser is targeting her store. That's rough, but it isn't me. If I have a problem with my ex-wife, I'll lay it on the line face-to-face. I wouldn't sneak around behind her back."

"You threatened to trash her car," Hale reminded him.

"I told her to be careful where she parked, that's all!" his friend flared. "Do you honestly think I'd stoop that low?"

"No." He could picture Joel smacking his fist against the hood in a moment of rage, or, as Connie had described, through a wall, but not planning a sneak attack. The guy was hot-tempered, was all.

Still, the image of him threatening her with a vase disturbed Hale. Even the *threat* of violence could cause trauma. And men were supposed to protect the women they loved, not intimidate them.

"Tell me she hasn't manipulated you into buying her crap," Joel added.

"Heck, no," Hale protested automatically. But wasn't entirely sure he meant it.

"She bats those blue eyes at men and they turn into marshmallows." Joel frowned into his half-empty beer.

"Gray," Hale corrected.

"What?" Joel frowned.

"Her eyes are gray."

"No, they're blue." A pause. "Maybe blue-gray." He regarded Hale assessingly. "You like her, don't you?"

"Somewhat." The admission slipped out.

A bitter laugh. "Yeah, she's alluring. Like a Venus flytrap."

The anger from Joel's failed marriage certainly hadn't dissipated. Still, Hale felt certain his buddy hadn't engineered the harassment.

Almost certain.

"I'm sorry." Skip stood at the bottom of the two steps leading down to the den. Connie, returning to the kitchen from dumping the after-dinner trash, studied him with apprehension.

"Sorry about what?"

Instead of responding, the little boy chewed his lip. Glancing past him, she surveyed the wreckage of her coffee table.

A toy truck Skip had brought from the Laytons's house, which he'd been playing with on the patio only minutes before, sat amid half a dozen scattered china figurines. A couple of others had fallen to the carpet.

"Let's see how bad the damage is." Struggling against an impulse to scold, she descended for an inspection, and then wished she hadn't.

A beloved shepherdess had lost her staff and one leg. The tail had broken off a darling little lamb. Worse, she doubted refinishing could remove the gouges in the shiny wood.

"I 'membered to take my shoes off." Skip's voice quavered as he indicated the sneakers on the entry mat.

Connie sank onto the sofa amid embroidered silk pillows, her stomach tight with dismay. Since childhood, she'd collected dolls and figurines, which to her represented a magic lacking in the real world. She'd assembled these statuettes and her delicate furnishings with loving care, creating a refuge from the disorderly world.

This hurt. But she needed to be patient.

"I'll pick up." Anxiously, her son righted a fallen shepherd with a multicolored cloak. "Pretty cape." His small fingers slipped, and the figurine toppled again.

In Connie's mind, a shrill cry of protest echoed. She recognized the near-hysterical tone from her childhood, the one her mother had employed when stressed. It used to make Connie shrivel inside, a feeling she didn't wish to impose on Skip.

Forcing herself to be objective, she surveyed the room. Gilt-framed photos crowded the bookcase, a porcelain vase and a crystal bowl topped an end table and beside the

DVD player she'd arranged candlesticks and etched-glass bottles.

Joel used to complain that he could scarcely breathe in this house. How *was* a boy supposed to act natural when every move threatened disaster?

Her vision of the room changed, as if the rays of sunset slanting through the French doors had shifted from pink to white. With newfound clarity, Connie saw not beloved *objets d'art* but, well, clutter. She hadn't stopped appreciating the craftsmanship or enjoying the delightful shapes. They still belonged in her bedroom and personal bath, and, of course, in her shop. But not all over a house she shared with her son.

Connie patted the sofa. Hesitantly, Skip approached, cringing when she reached to brush the bangs from his forehead. He must have endured a lot of anger in his former homes. "I'm not mad."

"You're not?" He wiggled onto the couch beside her.

"Grown-ups have to learn lessons, just like children." Her last hint of annoyance melted as she met his wide gaze. "I've never been a mommy before. You've taught me that this breakable stuff ought to be put away where it's safe."

"Can I help?"

A part of her shuddered at the prospect of allowing him to handle the vases and bowls and bottles. More pieces might get broken, and Skip would leave fingerprints all over the place.

When he's older, I might treasure those little reminders.

Connie tried to imagine her mother oohing over her own leftover smudges. Although she failed, she smiled at the notion.

Anna Farrar Lawson Rickards, a former actress, had lost none of her glamour over the course of five decades and two husbands. She still had her nails done weekly and, thanks to the miracle of plastic surgery, at fifty-seven appeared almost as young as her daughter. If she hadn't already possessed more than enough names, "Perfection" would have been the middle one. As for her south Orange County home, instead of the cozy but inexpensive arrangements that appealed to Connie, it featured designer furnishings that cost tens of thousands of dollars. And which hardly anyone ever sat on or ate at.

Connie hoped never to become that fussy.

Being around Skip reinforced her sense of what mattered: people rather than things. Compassion, not criticism.

"You bet you can help," she said. "We'll start tomorrow."

"Tonight!" Noticing her stern reaction to the demand, he added, "Please?"

He clearly longed to remedy the damage. How could she refuse?

"Let's drive over to the shop. I have boxes and packing materials in the storeroom." While they were clearing the den, she might as well remove some of the arrangements from the rest of the house. She could keep her favorites and take the other items to replenish the sale shelf at the shop. "I'm grateful to have an assistant like you."

"Yay!" The little boy ran to fetch his shoes.

In the lingering June twilight, Connie returned with her son forty-five minutes later bringing boxes, tissue paper and bubble wrap. She expected the joy of popping the plastic bubbles to sidetrack Skip, but he applied himself eagerly to packaging knickknacks. Although washing his hands failed to prevent a fair number of fingerprints, nothing broke and they toiled side by side like real partners.

They finished at about half-past eight. Connie, who'd been hurrying to complete the task before Hale arrived as promised, felt a rush of disappointment. He'd either forgotten or found something else that sparked his interest. The awareness that she'd deluded herself about his level of commitment to Skip only added to her disappointment. Thank goodness she hadn't informed the boy of the proposed visit. Adults had let him down too often.

But she herself had looked forward to Hale's presence. To his sense of humor, the rumble of his voice and the tingle of electricity she experienced near him.

The little boy drooped. When she announced bedtime, however, he proclaimed, "I missed my TV tonight. I want to watch *Narnia!*"

"When we have special activities, you can't stay up extra late to see a movie, too," she told him wearily. "Why don't I read to you from the Narnia books instead?"

"No!"

"Skip, I'm tired."

"Catch me!" He took off, little feet trotting down the hall. Even though she no longer had to brace for the crash of falling china, Connie barely hung on to her patience.

She'd put in a long day. She'd understood that exhaustion went hand in hand with motherhood, but, well, tonight was worse than usual.

Connie trailed Skip into the front room. "This isn't a game." Trying to be reasonable, she added, "Are you afraid of going to bed? I've arranged for you to see a doctor who gets rid of bad dreams." She'd set an appointment with Dr. Federov for Monday.

Instead of answering, the boy skirted a lacquered tray table and hurried across the room. Abruptly, he stumbled to a halt, gaze riveted on the door.

The knob was turning. She'd forgotten to lock it. "Who—who…?" The words stuck in Connie's throat.

An intruder. Before she could scoop up her son, the door swung open.

The tip of a cane appeared. "Something's wrong with your bell," Hale declared as he hobbled into view.

Skip ran to greet him. The two exchanged high fives.

Connie's knees threatened to buckle. She was incredibly glad to see him and, simultaneously, embarrassed by her momentary fear.

Shakily, she found her voice. "It didn't ring."

"Sorry I'm late. I fell asleep. You should lock this, by the way." He shut the portal behind him. "Thought I'd dispense with the crutches. Hey, Skip, my man, past your bedtime, isn't it?"

"I'm not sleepy!"

"Not in the mood for a super-duper night-night story from Detective Crandall, Super-hero?" An eyebrow waggled at the entranced youngster.

"Okay!" Skip aimed for the couch.

"Whoa, pardner!" Hale cast Connie a conspiratorial grin. "Got to have those pjs on and be tucked under the covers first."

Conflicting impulses seemed to war inside the boy. He didn't resist for long. "Don't go away!"

"I won't."

The little figure whisked off. In the bedroom, a dresser drawer scraped and slammed. A moment later, Connie heard water running in the bathroom.

"Thought I forgot, didn't you?" Hale said to her.

"You're not the most reliable man in the

world," she answered tartly, despite her pleasure at his arrival.

"When have I ever let you down?"

"When have I ever dared to count on you?" she riposted.

"No fair. You're confusing me with Joel." He crossed in Skip's wake. "I'll fix that doorbell just to prove what a good guy I am."

Much as she hated to concede the point, he was right—since Joel had often canceled planned activities and neglected household chores, she expected the same sort of behavior from Hale. Yet in truth he'd often come to her aid around the house and yard since the divorce.

"I appreciate it," she conceded. "And you're definitely not like Joel."

"Faint praise."

"Okay, I genuflect before your gracious munificence." She smiled.

"Better."

They heard Skip race to his room and moved down the hall to join him. They found him in bed with the covers pulled to his neck. "Ready!"

"Teeth brushed?" Connie asked.

A quick nod. She suspected he'd rinsed his mouth, at best. Despite the importance of dental hygiene, however, tonight his emotional needs came first.

"Got a favorite book?" Hale lowered himself onto the edge of the bed.

"Tell me a story!" the boy said. "Like, when you were a kid!"

That ought to be interesting, Connie thought.

"You sure?" Hale said.

Skip bounced on the mattress. "Yeah!"

"No bouncing," Hale warned. "You may be rubberized, but this superhero is still sore from tumbling two stories."

"I'm sorry."

"No problem." Hale shifted in place. "Hold on. I don't like this arrangement."

From the child-size desk chair where she'd wedged herself, Connie regarded the pair uncertainly. "What's wrong with it?"

"Face-to-face doesn't work." Stiffly, the man scooted alongside Skip, who wriggled into a sitting position. "Shoulder to shoulder, man to man."

"Yeah! Man to man!" Another bounce, quickly aborted. "Oops."

Hale leaned against the padded headboard. "How shall I start?"

"'Once upon a time,'" Skip prompted.

"Okay. Once upon a time a little boy named

Hale Crandall lived in a city called Fullerton. That's next to Villazon, where his dad was a police officer."

"Was he just like you?"

"Only bigger and tougher. Now, mostly this little boy acted like an angel, but once in a while he got into trouble. For example, when he was nine, he decided to hide a lizard in the teacher's desk...."

Entranced, the boy snuggled against him. What a sweet picture they made, the dark-haired man and the skinny, towheaded youngster, sharing a tale of mischief. Connie longed to gather them both in her arms.

What a scary feeling when applied to her neighbor! But it was only temporary, Connie felt...well, *almost* certain.

Chapter Nine

Hale didn't usually talk about his upbringing. However, after he finished the tale of classroom shenanigans, Skip's interest inspired him to reveal further details.

When the boy asked about his parents, he told the truth: that his mother had abandoned him when he was seven. In light of Skip's situation, the loss gave them more in common.

"So you don't have a mom?" Two round eyes peered at him.

"Basically, no. My dad brought me up."

"Do you ever see her?"

"Occasionally." When she'd filed for divorce after her departure, his embittered father had forbidden her to reestablish contact with their son, and for some reason she went along with it. After Hale entered college, she'd begun sending Christmas and birthday cards, and he'd visited her home in Las Vegas a couple of times since then, but they remained distant acquaintances. He presumed she maintained closer ties to her two grown daughters from her second marriage.

"Why'd she leave?" the boy asked.

Across the room, a pucker formed between Connie's eyebrows. Maybe she disapproved of the painful topic, or perhaps she was thinking of her father. Hale had heard she'd been raised by a single mother while her dad seemed totally wrapped up in his second family.

As for his mom, why *had* she fled? In Hale's father's view, Lita had been selfish, shallow and disloyal. As Hale grew up, however, he'd discovered that most stories had two sides. To his mom's credit, even years later she hadn't tried to excuse herself.

"I can't justify leaving you," she'd told him during a visit. "But your dad never stopped being a cop, not for one minute—at home, at work, with friends, with family. After our honeymoon, he rarely showed the sweet side I'd fallen in love with. I kept trying to please him until I couldn't stand it any longer. When I mentioned divorce, he got so mad he scared me. That's why I ran."

The situation reminded Hale of Connie and Joel. She'd left, too, but he felt certain she'd never have abandoned a child.

"She and Dad made each other unhappy," he answered the boy. "That happens to some grown-ups."

Skip struggled against a yawn. "But your dad stayed?"

"Absolutely." Unlike this little boy's, apparently. "At first, I thought maybe I'd driven my mom away because I broke the rules a lot. But that's not true. Kids aren't responsible for grown-ups' problems."

"I want to be good."

Touched by the plaintive note, Hale ruffled Skip's hair. "You're a wonderful little guy. No one expects you to be perfect."

"Certainly not me," Connie seconded.

The boy's eyes drifted shut. Gently, Hale slid him under the covers.

Connie waited by the lamp until Hale moved to the doorway. In the glow, tenderness softened her face.

Entering the hall, Hale glimpsed his reflection in a gilded mirror and noted that his indulgent expression matched Connie's. Skip might not be his son, but their time together meant a lot.

On the way to the living room, Hale's cane bumped a stand. To his relief, nothing fell, because the surface was bare. Didn't there used to be some sort of candle arrangement there?

The living room had changed, too. Same golden filigreed fire screen, same stiff sofa and ornate chairs, same painting of carnations above the mantel. But the welter of curios had vanished.

"What happened to the gimcracks?" he asked, amazed.

"The what?"

"The glass vases and china gizmos."

"We packed them. I can't expect Skip to mince around the house like a ballet dancer," Connie responded. "Wait. Ballet dancers leap and spin, don't they? Wrong comparison."

He laughed. "If you say so."

Connie sat in a chair and crossed her legs. As Hale took a seat opposite her, he wondered if other women still wore skirts around the house, and doubted many looked anywhere near as good in them.

They were getting along so well that he hated to spoil the mood. A smoother guy might have elaborated on the theme of shared parental concern, or steered the conversation to another polite topic, but he'd been raised with the finesse of King Kong. So his next words were, "I had a beer with Joel."

Connie hands curled into fists. "You asked him about the calls?"

"Yeah." Might as well cut to the chase. "He denies having anything to do with them."

"I hardly expected a confession." Her tone dripped sarcasm.

Hale refused to retreat. "The idea of pulling such a sneaky stunt offended him."

"I suppose he'd rather vandalize my car!"

"He was merely blowing off steam." Hale paused. He hadn't meant to defend the guy, only to present a balanced account. "I agree, he's got a nasty temper and a big mouth. I tend to assume his bark is worse than his bite."

Tight mouth, rigid posture. "I figured you two would stick together."

Faced with such marked opposition, Hale felt like bolting. Emotional conflict had always been high on his list of situations to avoid—yet why blindly follow a pattern just because he'd inherited it? "I'm not willing to fix on him as the suspect yet."

"Suit yourself."

Okay, he'd presented Joel's case enough. "Any further calls?"

"No." She relaxed slightly. "Maybe he'll back off now that you've spoken with him."

"I hope whoever's doing this tires of the game." *Because I'm certainly sick of it.* Outside, Hale noticed that darkness had fallen, but he hadn't forgotten his earlier offer. "If your porch light's strong enough, I'll have a go at that doorbell."

"Now?" She seemed pleased.

"Might as well."

"That would be wonderful. I'll fetch the tool kit." She smoothed her skirt as she rose. "Thanks for talking to Joel. I didn't meant to vent my irritation on you."

"What else are neighbors for?"

A few minutes later, as Hale set to work, he reflected that the disagreement he'd been tempted to duck hadn't turned out badly. Instead of accelerating into an argument, the discussion had eased tensions between them.

Staying the course and watching his attitude weren't easy on the ego. But although sniping at each other had worked when he and Connie were merely neighbors, that kind of behavior set a bad example for Skip.

Plus she was in such a good mood, she stuck around to watch him fix the loose wire. An optimistic fellow might suspect she enjoyed his company.

After providing a stool so Hale didn't have to stand on his sore ankle, Connie waited nearby in case he required anything else. She didn't want him to call out and wake Skip.

Besides, she liked watching his strong hands with their blunt-tipped fingers manipulate the wiring extracted from the wall. The attention to detail made her feel cherished.

Surprising how much she'd begun to rely on the man. For handyman tasks, for help with Skip and for the security of knowing he was there if she needed him.

Early in her three-year marriage, Joel had taken pleasure in assisting and supporting her. He'd grown less and less solicitous after the honeymoon phase, which she supposed was normal, but other problems had arisen: his refusal to compromise on issues large and small, coupled with his insistence on spending many evenings and weekends with the guys. Off-road vehicle riding, target shooting, video contests, attending Angels games—an endless list.

Connie had tried accompanying him, but perilous activities didn't suit her and, besides, most of the guys were single. She'd wearied of sitting alone or struggling to converse with their dates. After a while, she'd given up and scheduled her leisure activities with Marta and Rachel. Later, she'd devoted herself to the shop.

The mess at the police department, which dragged on for months, had widened the gap. Whatever pressures Joel had suffered, he'd vented them by complaining about almost everything she did or, in his view, failed to do.

If she'd known about the investigation in advance, Connie might have delayed opening her stores, but once she'd committed money and energy, she couldn't simply fold them. Besides, Joel's verbal sniping had eroded her desire to please him. He'd claimed she lacked loyalty, but loyalty cut both ways.

Without warning, he'd begun insisting they have a child. Maybe he'd assumed parenthood would save their marriage, but the demand had struck Connie as a strategy to restrict her independence. Since he refused to go to counseling, matters had deteriorated.

Hoping for the best, she'd waited until he'd finished testifying, hoping their relationship would improve. But when his mood and his attitude remained truculent, she'd consulted a lawyer.

Joel had resented the divorce, the alimony and her keeping the house despite reimbursing him for half the equity. He'd done his best to punish her by dragging his feet and partying next door. Now he'd sunk to new depths. Two years after she'd left, apparently her decision to adopt had fanned the flames of anger.

She hoped Hale's intervention had persuaded Joel to lay off. And that, if he didn't, Hale wouldn't side with her ex against her.

"All done." He stowed the tools and brought the stool inside.

"I'm so glad you fixed it. That's really kind of you." As she reached for the kit, her arm brushed his. Warmth sped through her out of all proportion to the lightness of the touch.

Common sense warned her to retreat and remove any hint of an invitation, but when Hale slipped an arm around her, she pressed close. Tilting her head up, she kissed the pulse at his throat and was thrilled to feel a shiver run through him.

He pulled her body against his so tightly that her hip felt his physical arousal. An urge to yield teased at her and in his eyes she saw that he, too, poised on a brink.

Before she could react, he stepped away. Connie's playboy neighbor, the man she'd always considered an easy conquest for any attractive single woman, had resisted temptation while she still wavered.

"I'm making an awkward effort to behave like a responsible adult," he explained regretfully. "We have Skip's interests to consider. And our better judgment."

Also how your best buddy would react if he found out you were sleeping with his ex, she thought. "And here I figured you'd take advantage if given half a chance."

"Well, don't press your luck," he responded.

She landed a mock blow on his shoulder. "That's a sample of what I dish out to presumptuous males."

"Could you do that on my back? It's sore from wielding that heavy screwdriver." He released an exaggerated sigh.

"Sure." When he swung around, she massaged his muscles briefly. "Only because you're still injured."

"I'm sore in a lot of places," he deadpanned.

"Sorry, soldier." She retreated a few steps

and deliberately brought up a neutral topic. "Skip's seeing Dr. Federov on Monday."

"I'm glad you took Russ's advice." He stretched. "The kid's endured a lot. What happened to his birth parents, anyway?"

"They had drug problems." Connie hadn't heard the whole story, but she'd learned enough to answer Skip's inevitable questions as he grew older. "In and out of jail, with no other relatives willing to assume responsibility. Eventually they lost custody."

"He's such a good kid. I hope he received some love along the way," Hale mused.

"I'm sure his mom did love him. Anyway, now he's got me. I plan to meet with Dr. Federov also, by myself, as well as with Skip. I want to prepare for his development at each stage."

Hale wore a thoughtful expression. "I never figured a parent would have to study child development. Seems like raising kids ought to come naturally."

"Maybe it does to some people." In fairness, Connie added, "You certainly have a knack for reaching Skip."

"Guess you'll have to invite me over more often to observe my technique." The glint of humor had returned.

"You're welcome to read to him whenever you like." She'd really like for him to become a regular fixture in the boy's schedule. The big brother he'd suggested.

"Appearing nightly. I like the sound of that."

"Done. If it's convenient," she added politely.

"Actually, it's fun. See you tomorrow." With a casual wave, Hale turned and hobbled outside.

Connie stood in the doorway, energized by the new accord between them. She scarcely recognized the man her neighbor had become since the fire, she reflected. Kind. Mature. The changes might be a temporary reaction to confronting his own mortality. But perhaps not.

As for the temptation she'd felt earlier, she was glad he'd called a halt. Marriage had taught her that treacherous shoals lurked beneath deceptively placid waters. Right now, she needed Hale as a friend too much to risk a volatile intimacy.

On Monday morning, Hale's return to the police department proved refreshingly anticlimactic. No reporters descended. No crises loomed.

Friday and the rest of the weekend had passed quietly. The ankle improved and the phone had rung occasionally with friends saying they'd read his name in the newspaper or glimpsed him on TV after the press conference. Several pals dropped by on Sunday for an impromptu barbecue and swimming party. Joel, however, kept his distance. Hale hoped the sore feelings would soon pass.

And he paid regular bedtime visits to Skip, whose fear of going to sleep had diminished considerably. Afterward, Hale always departed promptly. He sensed that any moves on his part were likely to alarm Connie.

Yet she had an influence on him anyway. Following yesterday's party, he'd spent half an hour collecting wrappers and cans, sweeping crumbs and storing the food, until a series of painful twinges reminded him to go easy. The problem, he decided, was that he kept noticing things that had escaped his attention before. Litter on the patio. A cigarette hole burned in his sofa. Not to mention the ugliness of his aging furniture. Well, no doubt he'd recover his normal indifference once the ankle healed and he could whiz past the mess the way he used to.

The Monday morning flurry of new files on his desk had the benefit of plunging his mind back into the job. A couple of robberies and several runaway teens all demanded resolutions.

Cases involving abuse and threats against women jumped out at Hale. He'd always been sickened by that spiral of violence, but today he probably found the reports particularly disturbing because Connie was being harassed. Fortunately, though, she hadn't received any further calls, a fact she attributed to Hale's words with Joel.

Hale didn't buy it. But he was grateful for the coincidence.

By late afternoon, he'd located a runaway girl safe at the Arizona home of her grandmother. The relieved parents booked a flight to Phoenix to collect her.

A robbery witness stopped by the bureau to provide additional testimony. Hale debriefed the man and, still limping a little, had just escorted him out when he spotted Connie at the front desk. Oh, man, why did his nervous system shift into high gear whenever she crossed his path?

"What's wrong?" He leaned on the counter.

She glanced past the desk officer toward the watch commander's office. "Is *he* on duty?"

He didn't have to ask whom she meant. "Day shift left an hour ago."

"Good." Tension and anger animated her tone.

"More calls?" he guessed.

"Worse." Leaving that ominous word hanging in the air, she added, "Skip's at Dr. Federov's office across the street, so I decided to walk over and file a report." She tapped a half-filled form.

"What do you mean by 'worse'?" Hale persisted.

She handed him a flier printed on yellow paper. It bore the misspelled name Conny's Curios, along with the store's address, and declared, "Fifty percent off all purchases!"

"Three customers brought these in today." She jotted further notes on the form. "He's progressed from annoying me to trying to bankrupt me."

Hale studied the flier. Anyone could have designed this on a computer. "Did the clients say where they got these?"

"Found them on their windshields this morning. They were parked on residential streets near the shop." She signed her name at an angry slant. "So far, there's no indication my other stores have been hit, but I have no idea how many of these Joel distributed."

"If it were him, he ought to be able to spell your name correctly," Hale pointed out.

"He gets it wrong all the time," she returned sharply.

"A customer might have dummied this up to get a bargain," he felt obliged to note. "Put a few on his neighbors' cars to deflect culpability."

"That's your expert opinion—that this is unrelated to the phone calls?" Connie demanded.

He couldn't support that position. "I'm only exploring possibilities. How'd you respond?"

She capped her pen. "I hate to alienate customers. I explained that I didn't authorize these but offered to knock thirty percent off a single purchase or fifty percent off any sale item."

"Gee, I'd go for that," he said.

"Thanks to Skip, I recently replenished the shelf. The candle arrangements went fast." She managed a weak smile. "Jo Anne had the idea of posting one of the fliers in the window with an explanatory note. The third person who arrived sympathized and told me a long story about problems with *her* ex."

"Did she request the discount?" Hale inquired.

"Well, sure. She wasn't *that* sympathetic." She regarded him sternly. "You aren't still siding with Joel, are you?"

"Completely objective." He nodded an acknowledgment to the desk sergeant, who collected the form. To Connie, Hale said, "This should be assigned to a detective in crimes against property. I expect you'll hear within a week."

"They ought to respond quickly, considering there's an officer involved," Connie returned.

"In the current climate, we're bending over backward to keep our noses clean." Hale decided he'd only rile her if he pointed out the unfairness of assuming Joel was guilty.

"How far do you suppose he'll go with this?" A glimmer of fear showed beneath the take-charge surface.

Hale's gut twisted. He hated seeing her upset. "I don't believe you're in danger. The man threatened your car, not your person."

"I'd stay at Marta's if it weren't for Skip." Connie's cousin occupied a studio apartment, too small for three people in anything short of an emergency. “Besides, I hate to be chased out of my home.”

“I’m next door. Call if anything worries you.”

She twisted a lock of hair around one finger. “I don’t want to believe it’s Joel, Hale. But I’ve racked my brain and there’s nobody else with a motive.”

“You never caught a shoplifter who might hold a grudge?”

That gave her pause. “Well, I suppose it’s possible, but with teenagers, I explain about being a small businessperson and how theft hurts me. If they’re contrite, I let them off with a warning.”

Enough on that subject, because a more interesting one had occurred to him. “If you’re worried, I’d be happy to sleep on your couch.”

“That’s very generous.” She considered briefly. “I have an alarm system, so I’m not *that* fearful. And I’d rather Skip didn’t assume you were living there. So, thanks, but I’ll decline.”

“Offer’s good for the duration. Anytime you get nervous, feel free to call.”

“I will. Meanwhile, let’s hope the wheels of

justice grind with all due speed." Her mood had eased noticeably. "See you tonight?"

"Eight o'clock."

She left to collect her son. Hale told himself he ought to be grateful he didn't have to sleep in her house tantalized by images of the woman of his dreams curled in bed only a room or so away.

The longer this harassment continued, the more torn he felt between his loyalty to his buddy and his concern for Connie's feelings. What he ought to do right now was back off, not draw closer.

With luck, maybe the detective assigned to the case would quickly identify a disgruntled ex-customer or rejected admirer and nail the guy's butt. That would suit Hale just fine.

Chapter Ten

For Connie, the week passed without further incident, although bogus fliers continued to trickle in. They mostly arrived in the hands of new customers, which was a benefit.

The technique appeared so successful that she hired a teenager to distribute similar fliers—offering a fifteen percent discount—in the parking lot near In a Pickle. The buoyant manager, Rosa, reported an uptick in sales.

Connie's harassment complaint was assigned to a young detective named Kirk Tenille. He interviewed her by phone and assured her he planned to question everyone who might have a motive. She hoped Joel would take a hint and knock off.

Skip showed less anxiety after two sessions of play therapy with Dr. Federov, and Connie learned some effective techniques for loving discipline. Thanks to Hale's support and continuing tales of his mischievous childhood, the boy now anticipated bedtime eagerly.

So did Connie. She kept an emotional distance between her and her neighbor, however. Too many issues remained, especially the matter of Hale's conflicting loyalties. Also, she still sensed that, deep inside, he remained a dedicated fun-seeking bachelor.

"Are you sure you're being fair? I mean, if he ever acts seriously interested, maybe you should give him the benefit of the doubt," Marta said one Friday night over dinner. "You have to admit you have trust issues."

They were sitting on the patio at a hamburger restaurant that had a play fort equipped with towers and slides. Skip, who'd finished his meal in a hurry, was clambering through a transparent tube in pursuit of another little boy.

Connie poked her salad with a fork. She'd have preferred a burger and fries, but every extra ounce showed in summer clothing. "This isn't about my father."

"Of course not," her cousin agreed. "It's about his total indifference to your feelings."

"I got over that ages ago!"

"Yes, by incorporating it into your mental world view. I wish I could give my uncle a good shake, but he's bigger than me." Marta downed a last bite of cheeseburger. Despite being only five foot one, she burned off calories with her high-energy personality.

"I wish I had your forgiving nature," Connie said. "You don't seem to mind the gifts your father lavishes on Aunt Bling." That was her nickname for her cousin's stepmother, Bryn Lawson.

"I'm just glad Dad's happy."

Connie couldn't help protesting. "Yes, but he ought to help you finish college instead of buying her jewelry!"

Her cousin sighed. "He figures I'm an adult and should manage my own finances."

Connie narrowly restrained a rude remark about her father's brother. He'd contributed to his daughter's support until she turned twenty-one and then stopped, declaring that she should rely on state aid while completing rehab.

After struggling to survive on a small disability check, Marta had landed a job cashiering at a discount store even though she shouldn't have spent so much time on her feet. When Connie acquired the hospital's gift concession, she'd immediately offered her cousin the manager's post and arranged the layout so that many tasks could be accomplished from a central desk.

Despite the passage of several years, Uncle Harry's callousness still rankled. "I hated watching Bryn remodeling their house, buying designer clothes and throwing money around while you were in pain!"

Marta rested her chin on one hand, light-brown hair swinging to her shoulders. Although the scars across her cheekbone and forehead had faded, they remained visible. "In rehab, I met a lot of bitter, angry people. Filled with rage about their bad luck or whomever they blamed for their condition. Resentment doesn't heal you, it festers."

"Well, I'm angry on your behalf!" Still, Connie admired her cousin's healthy attitude.

For herself, she didn't object to her father's absorption in his second family. He'd done his duty, diligently paying support to her mom even after he remarried. With his second wife, a glamorous Russian immigrant, he had two teenage sons.

Her dad, Jim Lawson, and his older brother, Harry, were a lot alike. Both good at finances, relatively humorless and lavish in their second marriages. Understandable for her own father after a divorce, but Marta's mother had died of cancer and Uncle Harry had no other children.

The thought of Aunt Bling stirred Connie's fierce protective instinct toward Marta. Her cousin was like a kid sister—although she was younger by a mere three months.

The table trembled as Skip dropped into his attached seat. "Thirsty!" he announced and sucked his soda through his straw.

"Refill?" Connie asked.

He shook his head. "Gotta go." Off he darted.

"He's a doll," Marta murmured. "I'm happy for you."

At the next table, a gray-haired man swung a toddler to the ground from a high chair. The two hurried toward the tot section of the play area. "Hurry, Grandpa!" the little girl cried.

"Fast as I can!" he replied jovially, and increased his stiff-legged pace.

The realization that her son would probably never enjoy a meaningful relationship with his new grandfather troubled Connie.

The boy really would benefit from having a father figure.

She pictured Hale, dark hair falling onto his forehead as he sat beside her son in bed, telling a story. If only…what? Too dangerous to let her imagination—or her heart—stray in that direction. She had to be satisfied with the arrangement they'd devised.

"There's something I need to talk to you about." Marta's words pulled Connie into the present.

That earnest note signaled a serious matter. "Is this business-related?"

"Sort of." A French fry disappeared down Marta's throat before she explained, "I'm planning to resume classes at Cal State part-time this fall. I'll be in my midthirties before I finish my B.A. and earn my teaching credentials, but at least I'm getting back on track."

Her life's goal of becoming a teacher had been cruelly interrupted by the accident. Neither her health nor her economic status had allowed her to return to school until now.

"That's wonderful!" Connie knew her cousin had been saving for this since returning to work. "Any possibility of a scholarship?"

"I found a partial one." Reluctantly, her

cousin added, "I'm afraid I'll have to change my hours."

"I'll be happy to accommodate you," Connie said.

"If you'd rather appoint a different manager, I'll understand," Marta offered.

"Are you crazy? No way!"

A relieved smile. "I hoped you'd say that."

In a companionable lull, Connie watched her son climb a short ladder behind his new friend. The thought occurred to her that neither she nor her cousin had focused their dreams on a man. They'd taken practical approaches that each promised plenty of satisfaction.

Not perfect bliss, but who could count on that? And when a weary Skip trotted over to throw his arms around her, she couldn't have asked for more.

On Saturday morning, the whine of a motor and a recurrent *whumping* woke Connie at seven-thirty. What the heck?

Emerging grumpily from the bed, she registered that the noise emanated from Hale's backyard, which she couldn't see from her bedroom window due to the intervening four-foot wall. If he'd decided to tune his off-road bike or all-terrain vehicle at this unholy hour, he deserved a dressing-down.

She pulled on a bathrobe and walked down the hall. Uncertainty replaced annoyance when a glance into Skip's room showed it empty.

No sign of him anywhere in the house and he failed to respond to her calls—which she had to shout over the din from next door. Growing anxious, Connie checked the front door. Locked and bolted. The rear exit from the family room, however, stood ajar.

Wishing she'd donned shoes instead of light slippers, she padded outside. A visual sweep of the emerald lawn and flower beds located a small figure standing on a chair, peering over the wall into Hale's territory.

Skip was safe. Although embarrassed by her tendency to panic, she found new grounds to worry: the evidence that, despite the heavy-duty lock she'd installed on the gate, Skip could clamber over with the aid of a chair.

Connie had read plenty of advice about supervising children, but none of it mentioned their resourcefulness. As Dr. Federov had noted, this boy was likely to challenge her at every step of his development. Still, she couldn't imagine a worthier mission.

Swiveling, Skip waved to her, lost his footing and flailed his arms. Connie flew across the grass, heedless of the damage to her slippers, but he regained his balance on his own.

"Look!" He pointed toward Hale's property. Resting one arm around him, more to reassure herself than to steady her son, she followed his gaze to the source of the clamor.

A workman was bent over the concrete, drilling a hole near the swimming pool. Two other men labored at the far end, kneeling to install hardware.

She'd requested a pool cover. Apparently Hale had arranged for that, plus a special enclosure, caring enough about her son to spend the money and chop up his backyard. She was impressed.

Into Connie's ear, Skip shouted, "What're they doing?"

She leaned close, enjoying the tickle of his hair on her nose. "Making the pool safe for you!"

"For me?" His eyes widened. "Can we go swimming now?"

"When they're finished," she promised. "If it's okay with Hale."

She shepherded the boy into the house, where he wriggled with excitement through breakfast. A trip to the library provided a welcome distraction.

Connie squelched the impulse to swing by her store. She'd hired a new clerk, whose schedule today overlapped with those of two other employees except for an hour or so when Paris had to run the operation alone. The three of them were perfectly competent, and Connie's weekends belonged to Skip now.

As she returned home shortly past one o'clock, a couple of workmen were stowing equipment in their vehicle. The racket had yielded to a peaceful afternoon broken only by the distant hum of cars and the burr of a lawn mower a few blocks off.

"Can we swim now?" Skip begged.

"I'll call Hale." Lugging a bag of books and borrowed DVDs into the house, Connie realized she'd be expected to join them. If she'd thought ahead, she'd have bought more conservative attire to wear than her pink bikini. Too late for that.

A message blinked on her machine. "In case the din this morning didn't give you a clue, my pool is transformed. Join me for a dip this afternoon." He hadn't bothered to leave his name.

Connie pressed the rapid-dial button. "Two o'clock?" she asked when Hale answered.

"Sure. That'll give us plenty of time. Derek and I are going to a movie at five o'clock."

She didn't ask which one. She didn't have to. She knew that an action thriller had just opened at a cinema complex in nearby Brea. A good bet the guys planned to see that rather than a romantic comedy or art film.

Skip ran to put on swim trunks. Connie retreated to her bedroom for the nerve-racking procedure of donning her swimsuit, which she hadn't worn in months.

Aerobics in front of the TV had kept her firm, she observed with satisfaction as she swiveled before a full-length mirror. She'd bought this skimpy pink two-piece after the divorce, when the whistles it drew at the beach had helped restore her self-esteem.

Connie surveyed the bikini again and felt a twinge of discomfort. Hardly the sort of thing a mother ought to wear, she decided, and pulled on a sari-style cover-up. Unfortunately, the robe was so gauzy it left little to the imagination. And Hale had a good one.

Enough dawdling. Since when did she worry about Hale's reaction, anyway?

Since he stopped acting like an overgrown

adolescent. And since you started finding him attractive.

Skip banged on her door. “Ready, Connie?”

Sticking her feet into flip-flops, she emerged, grabbed a couple of towels and a key, and escorted him through the rear yard. She was unlocking the gate when she realized she’d forgotten to bring sunscreen.

“We’d better…”

The scrape of a sliding door announced her neighbor’s emergence into the yard. “Come on through!” he called.

Connie ushered Skip inside and got an eyeful of tight-fitting trunks slung low on masculine hips. Despite remnants of bruising along his left side, he exuded his old brash confidence as he set out a cooler.

Bare chest, flat stomach, lightly furred legs and bare feet. When Connie had witnessed her neighbor in this state of near-nudity on previous occasions, she’d considered his raw sensuality an annoying sign of male arrogance.

That was before she’d spent night after night listening as he talked to her son. Before he’d assumed the unofficial role of guardian. Before she’d kissed him.

“Thanks for going the extra mile.” She indicated the tall fence, which dominated the space. "I suspect this arrangement puts a crimp in your entertaining."

"Nobody will complain. Besides, it's only temporary." Hale grinned. "Until Skip's a teenager."

Skip surveyed the fence, forehead puckering. "Open it! Please, Hale."

"Let's run a safety test," said their host. "Try to get through." To Connie he said, "There's also a cover with an alarm. I've retracted it, but if you'd like a demonstration, I'm willing."

"Not necessary." She didn't doubt that her neighbor had chosen an effective barrier.

The boy rattled the gate and fiddled in vain with the lock. When he attempted to climb, the fine mesh foiled the effort. In spite of the aid of a hard-resin chair, the height and the outward angle of the top blocked him, as well. "Can't do it."

"Good!" Connie applauded. "Skip, don't regard this as a challenge, okay? The fence is here to keep you and other kids from drowning."

"Pools are more dangerous than they appear," Hale added. "You can sink to the bottom and drown without making any noise. Never go in without an adult present, okay?"

"Okay."

The earnest response appeared to satisfy Hale. "Shall we get started on the swimming lesson?"

"Yes!" Skip pumped one arm into the air.

Sunlight spun his blond hair to near white, and his pale skin reminded Connie of her omission. "I forgot the lotion."

"Borrow mine." From a chair, he retrieved a tube labeled Kids' Sunblock. "Smells like bubble gum—I figured he'd like it."

He'd bought lotion for Skip? "That's perfect."

She applied lotion to the boy's face and torso. "Don't forget the big kid," Hale said when she'd finished, and took the place of the boy. "I can never reach the middle of my back."

"I'll do that section and leave the rest to you." Squeezing out additional lotion, she spread it lightly. Beneath her palms, the skin across his shoulder blades quivered. "Too cold?"

"Hot and getting hotter," he returned seductively, then said, "Scratch that. I'm not feeding you a line, okay?"

"You weren't?" Connie queried as she finished smoothing the cream.

"Consider it a knee-jerk reaction." Jokingly, he amended, "Or simply a jerk reaction. I developed a technique to use around women, and since it worked, I didn't bother to consider how juvenile it was."

Skip shook the fence. "Hurry up!"

"Sure thing, sport." To Connie, he said with a touch of pride, "Notice how quietly it rattles—that's because it's fiberglass. The only metal is in the latches and screws. That avoids the corrosion problem and it's safer in case of a lightning strike."

"Impressive." Even though Southern California suffered few electrical storms, the precaution seemed worthwhile.

Connie handed him the tube. With careless ease, Hale squirted out a dollop and smeared his face and chest without bothering to smooth the blotches. "Care to let me return the favor?"

She flashed on a sensual image of his hands moving over her body, smoothing the lotion onto her abdomen and along the edge of her bikini top. Dangerous territory, she thought with a delicious shiver. Her voice choked a little as she said, "I'll pass."

"Wise choice." With a wink, Hale went to undo the fence opening. "Now the professor swings into action."

She stretched on a chaise in the semi-shade of the patio cover and watched the two males cavort in the water. At first, they simply played in the shallow end, tossing a ball and riding on colorful floating devices called noodles.

When Skip's initial exuberance eased enough for him to settle down, Hale instructed him to hold the side of the pool, stretch out and kick hard. The splashing amused the boy, and he went at it with gusto.

Hale's patience with Skip impressed Connie. Joel used to grow restless whenever he'd tried to help her with the computer, or when she'd assisted on one of his projects. She couldn't picture him using that gentle voice with a child or repeating the same process over and over without chafing.

Lulled by the warmth and the murmur of voices, she let her eyelids drift shut. What seemed like seconds later, she awoke to a shadow overhead.

"Nice nap?" Hale was blocking her light.

"Not nearly long enough," she replied.

A rueful chuckle. "I figured for once I'd catch you without a quick answer. Guess you wake up ready for action."

Connie didn't want to discuss waking up anywhere near Hale. "What's in the cooler?"

"What're you in the mood for?" he countered.

"Diet soda." She sat up as he retrieved it. By the pool, Skip sat dangling his feet in the water and operating a remote-controlled boat. He laughed as it roared in a long, swinging arc. "You're generous with your toys."

Hale handed her a can and eased onto the adjacent lounger. "Stuff breaks sooner or later. Might as well enjoy it."

What a refreshing attitude, Connie thought, remembering her preoccupation with the figurines. Maybe she ought to adopt a little of it.

As she relaxed again, Hale's nearness and a delicious awareness of his body teased at her senses. She genuinely liked this man, to her amazement. Despite all obstacles, they'd developed a quirky but satisfying role in each other's lives. The one person she'd always considered unreliable had not only sneaked beneath her defenses but become the man she counted on most.

If her heart were the sole thing at stake, Connie might have risked letting him closer. But too many uncertainties remained. Too great a likelihood that he'd revert to form and disappoint both her and Skip.

She hoped not. Time would tell.

"I put doors on the kitchen cabinets," he said conversationally.

The remark interrupted her train of thought. "Excuse me?"

"After a couple of hinges broke, I left them open for convenience. They look better now." He took a swig of his soda before continuing, "But don't assume I'm turning domestic."

"Because your kitchen no longer resembles a war zone?" she teased.

"I vacuumed, too," he responded, sounding a bit miffed. "Derek finally returned my machine."

"Glad to hear it." Since he appeared to expect more of a response, she said, "You've changed, but I have to admit, I never really appreciated your strengths before."

"You didn't deserve your reputation, either," he replied.

Her hand slippery from lotion, Connie lost her grip on the soda. She caught it at the last possible instant. "What reputation?"

He looked as if he regretted the comment. "I don't want you to get mad."

Was he referring to her neatness fixation or something more serious? "Please explain."

"Forget I mentioned anything."

"Did Joel tell lies about me? I have a right to know!" She'd never suspected that other issues might affect Hale's impression of her.

His gaze fixed on Skip, who appeared to be weaving a story around the ship's movements. "Don't blame this on Joel. Remember, I spent plenty of time around you, too. I just used to consider you, well, self-centered."

"You mean selfish?" She searched for an explanation. "Because of the alimony?"

Clearly unhappy about the topic, he nevertheless dredged up an answer. "Money had nothing to do with it. I'm talking about loyalty issues with Joel."

That came as a surprise. "He claimed I cheated on him?"

"No!" Hale shook his head. "No, I meant that you didn't stand by him when he needed you."

The reproach jolted her. True, the disintegration of her marriage had accelerated during the period when Joel had to testify against Lieutenant Kinsey, but that was because her husband reacted to stress by becoming more critical and ill-tempered. Connie had tried to soften his moods, but ultimately concluded she couldn't knuckle under without surrendering both her self-respect and peace of mind.

"Maybe it looked that way to you," she conceded. "Maybe it truly felt that way to Joel. But I honestly tried to make it work."

"He claimed you didn't cut him any slack. Wait!" A raised hand halted her response. "Loyalty is especially important in a cop's wife, because we're under so much stress."

"I'm aware of that! Despite trying to get a business off the ground, I bent over backward to cook his favorite meals, to give him back rubs. And he took it for granted." Joel had rarely reciprocated, even though anyone could see Connie was bone-weary after hours on her feet.

"He's a little insensitive," Hale admitted.

"What drove me over the edge was his demand that we have a baby, as if parenthood was something you could impose on the other person instead of a loving decision you make together." Connie halted the recitation of old grievances. "Okay, I wasn't a saint and I'm sure Joel has some legitimate beefs. But I'm sorry you based your opinion of me on his perspective."

Hale regarded her ruefully. "I've always liked you, but I figured that deep down a man couldn't trust you in a pinch."

"You are so far from the truth I don't know where to start!" Connie burst out raggedly. "That's awful!"

Skip stopped playing to study them. With an effort, she reined in her distress.

"I meant to point out that you aren't like that any longer." Hale sounded apologetic, but hardly contrite.

"I never was!"

"How can a guy discuss things if you're going to hit the roof?"

"I was only defending myself!" She decided to stop before she got any more emotional. "We shouldn't argue in front of Skip."

"Well, when should we argue?" he asked with maddening calm.

The ringing of Connie's cell phone provided a welcome excuse to ignore the question. It was Paris, working alone.

"A bunch of people brought in a new flier!" she wailed. "It says we're knocking half off the sale items between three and five p.m., but the shelf's nearly empty! I found some overlooked Easter items and reduced them, but I'm running out."

Just when she'd begun to believe Joel might quit, he'd resumed his tactics. But despite her anger, Connie had to focus on the issue at hand. "How many people?"

"Eight or ten, and a couple of teenagers are entering as we speak."

Far too many customers for one person to handle alone. Connie blamed herself for leaving a gap without two salesclerks on a Saturday. Since neither of the other employees had been available, she should have planned to cover it.

Her watch showed 3:20 p.m. Jo Anne couldn't arrive until five; she had a previously scheduled party at which she was selling cosmetics.

"I'll fetch more merchandise." Perhaps the other two shops had excess items. "I'll be there in half an hour. Can you hold the fort?"

"I'll do my best."

Connie explained the situation to Hale while she collected Skip from the pool. Some of her irritation with her neighbor dissipated when he offered to cancel his plans and watch the boy, but she preferred to reserve such favors for occasions when she had no alternative.

"He can stay with me. I'll only be at the

store an hour or so," she responded. "Thanks, though."

"Call if you change your mind." He sounded regretful. Surely he and Derek wouldn't enjoy watching a G-rated movie, however, and the action movie was too violent for a kid.

Also, Connie preferred not to let Derek or any of the other officers believe she was imposing on her neighbor. She wondered how many of them had entertained the same negative impression of her as Hale. Rachel had never mentioned it, but then they were old friends.

She hoped they'd all change their minds when they discovered what a jerk Joel had become. As Connie hurried Skip through the gate, she realized she ought to report this latest infraction to Detective Tenille. That would have to wait, though, while she contacted her other stores both to make sure they weren't suffering similar problems and to determine whether they had excess stock she could collect.

No matter what tactic Joel pulled, she refused to let him harm her business. One of these days, he'd have to admit defeat. And, she hoped, go down in flames.

Chapter Eleven

While storing pool toys in the garage, Hale replayed the conversation with Connie. Had he really accused her of being selfish and disloyal? He should have kept his mouth shut.

He'd almost compounded the error by defending Joel. That would have been doubly offensive in light of the latest prank regarding her shop.

Who the heck *was* doing this, and why? Although Hale maintained his faith in his friend, he wished the case had been assigned to a more experienced detective. Tenille tended to go by the book, in which Suspect Number

One was generally the alienated ex-boyfriend or ex-husband.

Impatiently, he locked the pool fence and went to dress for the movies. Joel had declined the get-together without specifying why. That didn't mean he had anything to do with the new fliers, of course. In fact, if he'd been trying to cover his tracks, he'd have distributed them earlier and then showed up acting as if nothing were afoot.

Today's development struck an odd note, though, perhaps because the offering of a discount was repetitious. Why would the guy repeat a strategy that Connie obviously knew how to counteract?

During the drive to the theater, uneasiness dogged him. Why specify particular hours for the bogus sale? Perhaps the culprit had learned that a clerk would be on duty alone, thus providing an opportunity to cause maximum confusion—but that presumed an inside knowledge of the store's employee schedule. Vince Borrego visited often enough to have overheard such plans. Also, he remained potentially implicated in the fire at Ben's. Well, his name had made Tenille's list, Hale recalled, so if he really was involved, the detective ought to be able to figure that out.

Reaching downtown Brea, he parked on the third level of the structure behind the movie theater. Approaching the elevators, he gathered from the knot of waiting filmgoers that several pictures must be starting shortly.

A crowd. Like the one Connie's clerk must be dealing with, thanks to the narrow time period for the sale. What if the goal wasn't to create an annoyance but a distraction? Perhaps the perp had a goal beyond mere harassment. But what?

"Waiting for someone?" Derek inquired. Startled, Hale realized his friend had strolled up and caught him standing motionless as the elevator doors shut.

Good. He needed objective feedback on his possibly over-the-top speculation.

"There's been another incident at Connie's Curios and I'm concerned. I could use your input."

"Yeah? What's going on?" Ignoring the arrival of a second elevator, the information officer folded his arms and stood listening as Hale outlined the situation and his suspicions.

When he finished, Derek shared his concern. "You should call and warn her now!"

"Right. Ask Dispatch to send someone as a precaution, will you?"

"Gotcha," Derek said.

Hale's hands shook so badly it took several attempts to hit the right button on his phone. Connie's cell went straight to a message. He tried the shop but found the line busy.

"I'm going to drive over there," he informed his friend.

A nod. Derek was on the line with dispatch.

Hale hoped they were overreacting. He hated to speculate about what sort of trouble the creep might perpetrate in a crowded shop.

Limping along the ramp toward his car, he tried to ignore the pain in his ankle. Behind the wheel, he covered the four miles to Villazon slightly above the speed limit and skimmed through a couple of yellow lights. Fear knotted inside him for Connie and Skip.

The blare of a siren burned a path through his nervous system. What was it responding to?

As Hale passed the supermarket and the discount furniture mart, he spotted a flashing light in front of Connie's Curios. Unreality enveloped him as he took in the scene: two black-and-whites with roof-mounted light bars activated, and a fire truck, possibly a backup for paramedics.

Something *had* happened. He felt a knot of fear and an agonizing blast of disbelief.

A handful of people, several clutching the store's signature red bags, milled about on the sidewalk. An officer guarded the doorway, while another stood fielding questions from Tracy Johnson, who must have walked over from the *Villazon Voice* office.

He didn't see Connie and Skip. Were they all right?

His throat tight, Hale parked and headed for the shop front. He paused at the sight of Rachel Byers sitting in her patrol car making notes.

"Rach!" He braced against the car. "What's going on?"

Clear hazel eyes fixed on him. "Yo, Hale. It's food tampering."

"It's what?" This was a gift shop, not a restaurant.

"Someone messed with the candy bars."

Food tampering could kill people. "Anyone hurt?"

"Unknown at this time." She swung out of the car. "According to Connie…"

"You talked to her? Where is she?"

"She took Skip to the hospital, just in case," Rachel replied evenly.

"In case of what?" he demanded while registering facts: Connie was fine. But Skip might have ingested something. "Did he feel sick? Any sign of shock?"

"According to Connie, he got upset when she refused to let him finish the bar. That's all." She tapped her pen against the pad. "Simmer down and let me explain."

"Okay, okay." Hale tried to regulate his breathing. "Get to the point, okay?"

"Don't I always?" she replied.

His comments were only delaying matters, he saw. "Okay. I'm listening."

She ran through her notes, hitting the highlights. Connie had arrived with a box of sale goods and got busy helping the clerk. When Skip requested a candy bar, she'd agreed. As he ate, she'd noticed that the candy display was a mess, and chided the boy.

"He denied doing it. She assumed a customer had been careless and started to straighten up. That's when she discovered that several appeared to have been unwrapped, then rewrapped."

"Rewrapped?" Hale repeated.

"Yeah. Somebody substituted a couple of cheap bars for the fancy imported stuff she carries. Skip ate half of one." Rachel grimaced. "What kind of creep picks on kids?"

"What was in it? How's Skip?"

"Seems fine so far, but they have to empty his stomach as a precaution. I called Russ. He doesn't usually work in the E.R., but of course he'll take care of Skip." A pediatrician with an office in the Mesa View doctors' building, which was next door to the medical center, her husband had hospital privileges. "The cheap bars contained peanuts and the original ones didn't. Luckily he doesn't appear to be allergic."

Although Hale had heard of contamination involving food items and over-the-counter medicines, substituting one product for another seemed bizarre. "Too complicated for someone to have engineered the switch in the store, so the perp must have brought the phony bars onto the premises."

"Planned in advance," Rachel concurred.

Hale didn't believe Skip had been targeted personally. Anyone might have eaten that candy. So there must have been a more complex motive than inflicting harm. "Did the clerk receive an extortion demand?"

"She claims not. Detective Tenille's on his way here now to look into it." She blew out a breath. "Lots of people wandering through when I arrived, thanks to those fliers. Clerk says a couple of people bought candy bars, but she doesn't recall anyone in particular poking through them."

Hale no longer doubted that the two-hour sale period had been arranged as a diversion. "Whoever did this set it up carefully. He must have cased the store in advance to make sure there was no surveillance camera." The parking lot didn't have one, either, he noted. "This isn't the work of a teenage shoplifter."

"I agree. Uh, Hale?"

"Yes?" he asked, studying the layout of the area in the hope it might yield a clue or that he might spot someone suspicious watching the scene. Criminals often enjoyed hanging around the area, relishing the results of their work. It gave them a sick sense of power.

"There's one more thing." The words seemed dragged out of Rachel. "I found this on the floor." She hefted an evidence bag. The business card inside showed a shoe tread, as if stepped on. It also carried the engraved Villazon city seal, the words *Police Department* and, in the center, a name: Sgt. Joel Simmons.

Hale's gut twisted. Still, he recalled, officers printed their own cards on stock provided by the city. "Someone might have forged this."

"Had to be another officer or city employee. Who else has access to the embossed stock? But that seems so unlikely." Rachel's rueful tone reflected the fact that she, too, liked their colleague.

"Unless he's gone off his rocker, Joel wouldn't pull a stunt like this." Hale felt certain.

"Some guys go nuts where their ex-wives are concerned," Rachel countered.

"Joel claims he's being framed. Possibly to embarrass the department."

"I hear there's a lot of that going around," remarked a dry female voice. Tracy Johnson, who was so short the cruiser had hidden her approach, rounded it. "What's this about Joel, by which I presume you mean Connie's ex-husband?"

Rachel slipped the card out of sight. Hale could have kicked himself for speaking so loudly.

"Being her ex automatically makes him a person of interest," he told the reporter. Useless to protest against her snooping. Although they'd been conducting a private conversation, they were standing in a public place, so were fair game.

Tracy turned to Rachel. “I hear you were the first officer to respond. Did you see anyone suspicious?”

“We’re interviewing everyone present at the scene,” Rachel replied blandly.

Without bothering to excuse himself, Hale made his way back to his vehicle. He preferred to speak to the press as little as possible, and since this wasn’t his case, the woman had no reason to question him.

On the drive to the hospital, he reviewed the latest developments. If the object had been to hurt Connie financially, the food tampering should have occurred at In a Pickle, which stocked more edibles. Candy constituted only a fraction of the sales at the main store.

Dropping a business card was a stupid move, and atypical of a man like Joel. To Hale, it smelled like more of a setup, which brought his suspicions back to Vince. But what about the still-unidentified man Yolanda had glimpsed before the fire?

No one came to mind. He was too preoccupied with worrying about Skip. If the boy *had* swallowed poison or drugs, he might be convulsing, going into shock…

* * *

Whoever had done this to her son, Connie hated him forever. In order to protect Skip, she had to approve unpleasant procedures that forced him to suffer regardless of whether the candy turned out to be harmless.

The one bright spot was Rachel's husband. A low-key doctor with black hair graying at the temples, Russ McKenzie had put her and Skip at ease while a nurse started an IV with fluids to flush out toxins.

The needle prick became merely the start of the misery. Skip had to swallow a substance that made him throw up. Later, he washed down a nasty black powder called activated charcoal to neutralize drugs and toxins. Next came a fluid called magnesium citrate—which tasted disgusting, Skip said—to further clean him out.

In a cubicle off the E.R., he huddled against Connie on a gurney while waiting for the citrate to take effect. "I hate that stuff," he whined. "And I hate chocolate."

"Don't blame candy bars." She didn't wish to deprive him of an occasional source of pleasure. "A bad person messed with that one."

She couldn't bring herself to speak Joel's

name. Didn't want to believe that he had done something this cruel. Terrifying to consider that he might truly have gone over the edge.

At the shop, Rachel had offered a temporary restraining order against him, but Connie had declined it. What use was a piece of paper against an armed man? Worse, she'd read of such orders infuriating the subject to the point of violence. She'd decided to wait and discuss the matter with her attorney.

Russ popped in again. "How're you two doing? As long as I'm here, I checked on a twelve-year-old surgical patient upstairs. He's doing fine."

"I'm glad." Connie's heart went out to the child. And his parents. "Who's watching Lauren?" Guiltily, she reflected that, with Rachel on duty, he'd had to make arrangements for his daughter.

"My mother and father picked her up for an overnight visit, as planned. Doting grandparents," he added fondly.

"Skip hasn't met my mom yet." Connie preferred to postpone that encounter until she felt more settled. "Have you, sport?"

Skip kept silent, leaning against her with a hangdog expression. His unusual droopiness intensified her self-blame. If only she'd left him with Hale or watched the boy more closely. This little boy had trusted his well-being to her and she'd failed him.

"We appreciate your coming in," Connie told the physician. "Hospitals are scary places."

Thanks to Russ, she hadn't had to worry about being questioned by a physician unaware of the harassment case. She was in no mood to have to persuade the medical personnel that she hadn't somehow caused this problem herself. Especially so early in the adoption proceedings, any blot or question on her record might present a serious obstacle.

"Being a parent isn't easy." Russ smiled. "Especially when you walk into it blindfolded."

"Not many folks would understand."

"At least you and Skip had a relationship," he replied. "Lauren and I were strangers."

He'd taken on a child with even less warning than Connie had had. Years before, when his girlfriend became pregnant during his internship, he'd complied with her wish to yield custody to her parents. Although he soon regretted the decision, he'd respected the grandparents' insistence on barring him from Lauren's life.

Five months ago, the grandparents had died in a small-plane crash. On learning that his ex-girlfriend didn't plan to raise their daughter, Russ had stepped into the breach and enlisted Rachel's help on a temporary basis. When love bloomed between the sophisticated doctor and the down-to-earth cop, the transitional family had become permanent.

"When can I go home?" Skip asked plaintively.

"You have to hang around so we can observe you. In case you get sicker or turn into a tiger or grow wings." Russ's attempt at humor failed to bring a smile.

"How long?" the boy asked.

"At least a couple of hours, maybe overnight."

"No!" A spark of the old forcefulness flared. "I won't stay!"

Connie squeezed him gently. "Listen to the doctor, sweetie." Although she shared his dislike of hospitals, she dreaded taking him home. Today's events had thrown her off-kilter, raising new fears. *Maybe I'm not tough enough or smart enough to be his mother. Maybe I'll sleep too deeply and won't hear him call out.*

"So far he hasn't shown any abnormal

symptoms," Russ conceded. "I could release him in a few hours if he's still doing well."

A tap at the door frame drew their attention to Hale. Skip uttered a cry of welcome and Connie's spirits leaped.

"That sounded like good news, right?" Hale said. "Something about no abnormal symptoms, right, Doc?"

"That's correct." Russ shook hands with the new visitor. "Good to see you."

"Take me home!" Skip pleaded.

"Depends on what the doc says," Hale told him.

Russ considered. "As I was saying, I'm willing to let him go later tonight if he's feeling okay and if his mother approves."

Two hopeful male faces focused on Connie. She *would* rather take her son home if she could count on Hale's support. "Are you still willing to sleep over in the guest room?"

"Sure. In fact, a sleeping bag on the floor is all I..." He stopped, then finished with a touch of embarrassment, "All I used to need before I took a flying leap into the stratosphere."

"Sleep in my room," Skip begged.

"The guest room will be perfect *if* the pretty lady is willing to remove a few hundred gewgaws from every available surface so I don't crash into them during the night," Hale teased.

Connie could have slapped him. And hugged him. "Most of them are gone already. I'll remove the rest." Then, ironically: "We could use them on the store's sale shelf. It's depleted again."

"That's settled," Hale concluded. "Okay, fill me in. What's this sawbones been doing to my favorite little guy?"

"Making me barf," Skip volunteered. "It's yucky!"

"You think that's bad?" Hale took a chair. "Guess what the toxicologist is going to do with the contents of your stomach? Poke through it! How'd you like that job?"

"Gross!"

Hale proceeded to describe the tests to be run, destroying the appetite that Connie had developed but delighting Skip and amusing Russ. The flat lighting took on a sparkle as their visitor jollied his young friend.

"How long before we get the results of all these lovely tests?" Connie asked Russ.

"Probably a few days."

Smoothly, Hale changed the subject, regaling Skip with a silly story that had them all laughing.

With her neighbor around, the world didn't feel nearly as threatening. Connie forgave him for his hurtful words that afternoon.

A while later, Jo Anne phoned to say the police had finished their inspection and released the store to her. "I gave them the remaining candy as evidence, but I bet they'll eat it," she joked.

Connie glanced at her watch. Nearly seven—closing time. "Would you mind setting a few items on the counter so the gap isn't obvious?"

"Already did."

"I'll understand if you and the other staff are nervous about working for me." Connie hated broaching the subject, but she was responsible for her employees' safety. "There's no telling what he'll try next. If you'd rather stay home for a while, I'll run the place alone or…" The words trailed off.

A steely note entered Jo Anne's voice. "We are *not* going to let this creep ruin things for all of us."

A lump formed in Connie's throat. "I can't tell you how much I appreciate your dedication."

"Dedication?" Her assistant snorted. "Paris

and I wouldn't give up these jobs for the world! Employers willing to schedule around college classes and cosmetics parties aren't exactly a dime a dozen."

All the same, she thanked Jo Anne again. Now if only the police could find the evidence to charge Joel, she'd gladly put this episode behind her.

For tonight, though, she relied on Hale's comforting presence to heal the jitters. For both Skip's sake and her own.

Chapter Twelve

Hale awoke in the early morning darkness with his feet sticking out from beneath the covers. Bed too short, mattress too firm. Dimly, he remembered arriving at Connie's house late in the evening after the hospital finally released Skip. During the few minutes Hale had required to fetch his pajamas and toothbrush from next door, the boy had fallen asleep.

Hale, too, must have nodded off almost instantly once he inserted himself between the crisp sheets. Since Connie had set the burglar alarm, he wasn't attempting to play watchdog. He'd stayed here to provide reassurance, and defense if the shrill alert failed to dissuade an intruder. Having a cop in the house beat the heck out of waiting ten minutes for a patrol car.

Through the partly open door of his room came a soft whimpering. Perhaps that was what had awakened him.

Hale swung to his feet, flinching as twinges assaulted his body. He'd forgotten to bring slippers, but, grubbing around on the floor, located his socks.

When he padded into the hall, he heard a restless muttering. To his surprise, it came not from Skip's room but from Connie's. Yesterday's events must have precipitated a nightmare.

He hadn't entered the master bedroom since before Joel brought his bride home. The house had gone up for sale about a year after Hale purchased the one next door, and he'd promptly notified his about-to-be-wed buddy. Hale had swung through here with Joel and Connie before the purchase, but on subsequent visits had avoided the boudoir. Even an accidental glimpse through the window once while helping Connie with yard work had felt inappropriately intimate.

Floral fabrics and French-style furniture. Enough china and crystal bottles and vases on the dresser to stock a dining room. Girlie stuff, his dad would have termed it. To Hale, the old-fashioned array hinted at an entirely different woman beneath Connie's usual brisk manner—one capable of great passion.

A passion she had only shared with Joel.

A soft cry broke through Hale's reverie. He set out down the hall to fulfill his promise to rescue Connie, if only from a dream.

Passing the boy's room, he glanced in. Covers were bunched around Skip, but he was breathing evenly. In the circle of light from a lamp purposely left on, his color appeared good. As Russ had affirmed, there was no sign he'd ingested drugs or poison. Still, for an allergic person, the outcome of consuming that mislabeled candy bar might have been deadly.

Surely Joel hadn't been responsible. Joel, whose house this used to be. Joel, whose role as protector Hale had assumed.

He shuffled onward, to the threshold of Connie's room. A sweet scent—lavender? lilac?—invaded his senses as he entered. Despite the dimness, crystal dangles around a lamp caught a glimmer of moonlight from a rear-facing window.

On the queen-size bed, Connie stirred fretfully. Hale reached toward her, his hand stopping just short of the tangled, pale hair.

He'd pictured this scene many times, but despite the familiar components—the woman, a bed, himself—this was different. In the past, Hale had whipped up a pretend version of her, a lovely, problem-free projection of his desires. Yet standing here now listening to her breathing, he saw a complex individual, vulnerable and trusting. In a silky slip-type nightgown that left her shoulders bare, she looked so fragile that he hesitated to touch her. Then a faint sob escaped her lips, and his fingers tapped her arm. "Wake up."

She thrashed sharply. "What?" she asked in a dazed voice.

"Bad dream," Hale murmured.

Connie sat up sharply and tugged the quilt around her. "What are you doing here?"

"Protecting the house against demons, real or psychological," he reminded her. "You were tossing and moaning, so I figured I'd do you a favor."

She pressed a button on the headboard to activate a low-level sconce on the wall. Soft light caressed the sheen of her gown and the tiny embroidered flowers across her breasts. "I was searching for Skip in the shop, only it seemed enormous. Each time I spotted him, he would dart into another aisle. That's all I remember."

"You're afraid of losing him," Hale remarked.

"Not hard to interpret, huh?" she said.

"It's a parent's worst fear." During his years on patrol, he'd helped hunt for several lost children. He clearly recalled the fear on their parents' faces.

Connie drank from a bottle of water on the bedside table. "On TV, single parenting appears to be a breeze. You dispense love and wisdom in equal measures and the kids' mischief always turns out well. And some of the parenting books aren't much better. They tell you to never let the child out of your sight, but how is that possible once they reach Skip's age?"

"You can't keep a six-year-old in a padded cell." With her permission, Hale sipped from the bottle to clean out his own vestiges of sleep. Lemony with a trace of sweetness.

"I'm not sure I can handle this alone," Connie confided wistfully. "The more I learn about kids, the more I realize how hard it is to provide everything they require. I feel so inadequate."

"So if you were, say, married, you'd instinctively have noticed that someone had tampered with the chocolate bars?" Hale inquired. "Or would you and your hubby follow your kids around like bloodhounds, making sure they don't so much as breathe without your consent?"

She uttered a sound halfway between a chuckle and an impatient cluck. "Don't be silly!"

"Listen to an experienced cop," he advised. "Watchfulness pays, but no parent is omnipotent. Plus, as kids grow, you have to gradually loosen the reins. Neglect them and they'll run wild, but clamp down too hard and you've got an angry, rebellious teenager." He hadn't realized until now that he'd observed that much.

"You've thought a lot about kids." Connie indulged in a small yawn, a movement that pulled the fabric suggestively across her breasts. "Hale, I'm just discovering how little I know. Where'd you learn all this, anyway?"

"Not from my dad," he admitted. "In a way, I parented him. Scolding him about drinking. Telling him to fasten his seat belt. That kind of stuff."

"Hale the caretaker," she murmured. "Mr. Mom, junior."

"Not really. You couldn't have eaten off our floors unless you were a dog."

She laughed. "You couldn't have eaten off ours, either, because my mother would have had you arrested."

He seized the chance to ask about a subject that intrigued him. "What happened to your dad?"

"My folks divorced shortly after my tenth birthday." When the covers slipped a few inches, Hale's eyes flew to the curves beneath the flimsy nightgown. Firmly, he looked away. "Dad later found a beautiful Russian woman on the internet. Considerably younger than he is."

"How'd that work out?"

"To our astonishment, rather well." Sleepily, she rested her head against the carved headboard. "Dad caters to Mila's taste for glamour and, unlike my mother, she appreciates him. I have two half brothers in high school."

"So you're on good terms?"

"More or less. We're not close, though." Connie blinked. "Wow. I got teary all of a sudden."

"Why?"

"Because…because my dad never loved me. The only times I got his attention were when I did something that embarrassed him. Like once when we ran into each other at South Coast Plaza. I was giggling and clowning with my friends in the food court, and I looked up to see him staring at me like...like he wished I'd drop off the face of the earth. Then he just turned and walked away with Mila. He didn't even say hello.

"And one time I fell off my bike and had to have stitches. Mom called and left him a message, but he never phoned back. Not a life-threatening injury, but it shook me up." She wiped the corner of her eye. "What a contrast to the way you rushed to the hospital today for Skip. And stayed over tonight so we wouldn't be frightened."

"I don't deserve credit for following my instincts." He'd never have slept well at home for wondering how they were.

"Well, even in this short time period, you've been more of a father to Skip than Dad was to me." She spoke with such sadness that Hale wanted to comfort her. But when he reached forward to hug her, a pain in his side made him flinch.

She saw it. "Turn around. I'll rub your back."

An irresistible offer, and he gathered she intended to do a more thorough job than she'd offered following his doorbell repair. He shifted so that his back faced her. Unexpectedly, she straddled him from behind, arousing a restless yearning. The pleasure he felt was so keen he suspected she must have noticed his reaction, but she didn't withdraw.

Deft fingers probed his neck and spine, teasing his muscles into submission. Heightened awareness coupled with a powerful sensual drive flowed through him. "You're good at this," he rasped.

"I studied massage to help Marta through rehab." She explored the tightness between his blades. "You're hard as a rock."

To his embarrassment, a moan emerged. *If she only knew the half of it!*

"Don't get ideas." Obviously she'd interpreted his response correctly.

"Furthest thing from my mind." Okay, not true. Surely she could tell she was stimulating nerve endings that had no connection to his muscles.

Hale willed himself to say he'd better return to his room. Couldn't squeeze the words out, so he rolled away, scrounged the strength to launch himself to his feet and stumbled inelegantly toward the exit. His body protested at every level.

So near to paradise. Thank goodness he had the strength to resist, by the thinnest of margins.

"What do you think you're doing?" Connie asked.

Hale froze. Had he really heard an invitation in her voice? If he turned, one glimpse of her face in the lamplight might destroy what remained of his resolve. "Behaving myself?"

No answer.

"Closing the door?" he tried.

"Better."

He summoned his nerve. "Locking the door?"

"Better still."

Hale performed that task and swung around. Blond hair spread across the pillow, covers draped across Connie's chest. The scene looked exactly as he'd imagined. But he was no longer the carefree rascal of those fantasies. "Are you sure about this?"

"What would it take to convince you?" she inquired sweetly.

He remained motionless. "I've had these—" he cleared his throat "—X-rated previews, starring you. But I couldn't reach the point of..." He gathered his courage. "Seeing you naked."

Unexpectedly, she laughed. "You had sexual fantasies in which you didn't dare take my clothes off?"

"I said previews. Not the whole movie." Now that he'd admitted the awkward truth, Hale decided to press onward. "If you're serious, go that extra step for me, will you? Then I'll know this is real."

He held his breath. Hoping. Ready. Conscious that if he'd overstepped, they might never again go this far.

She dropped one of her thin straps. Favored him with a teasing half smile and slowly eased the satin gown from beneath the covers. She pulled it over her head and tossed it to the side.

He still could see only the tops of her breasts. Perfect and magical, but…

She lowered the quilt, inch by tantalizing inch, revealing two perfect orbs, followed by a slim waistline with a very provocative navel, and wispy black panties. Darn, he'd forgotten to breathe. When he did, Hale swung into action.

"Let me help you with the rest." He crossed the room, sank reverently beside her and gazed appreciatively at the full breasts, their pale tips erect. Yet, he discovered, he was far more fascinated by the tenderness shining in her eyes.

Hale's lips met Connie's as she sank to the pillow. After all these years, he understood why his brain hadn't been able to manufacture this experience—not because of guilt but because what he craved surpassed the physical.

Now he was about to discover exactly what he'd been missing.

Connie reveled in the freedom of opening to Hale. How heavenly to touch him at last, to feel his mouth move against hers, to feather the hair on his neck as she cradled him. What fun to undo the buttons on his pajama top and tease his chest with her tongue. Each groan from him stimulated her further.

She luxuriated in arching to him. Crazy, maddening, virile Hale. She'd been battling this guy and her instincts for years. Tonight, she'd lost the will to fight.

He whispered in her ear. An endearment? Didn't sound like one. "What?"

"Protection," he repeated.

Oh, yes. She hadn't had occasion to use any since her divorce. "Might be—check the drawer." *Please let there be that one trace of my marriage remaining.*

He fumbled around and found it. While he opened the package, she tugged down his pants to find him ready. And so incredibly dear, with wonder written across his face at her boldness.

Connie stroked Hale lightly. Watched him succumb, fall back atop the mattress and lose himself in sensation. A delight for her, too, to slide the condom onto his hardness. Then she stretched out and kissed him, relishing the control of being on top. Almost before she was ready, Hale caught her hips and united them with one powerful thrust. Ecstasy filled her, although she wasn't nearly ready to climax.

Or didn't believe she was. But when Hale moved, the length of him stimulated her almost past bearing. She wanted to hold on, to delay so she could relish each second, yet could hardly tolerate the suspense.

Brilliant colors danced through Connie. Eager to explore, she licked the pulse of Hale's throat and nuzzled his rough cheek with her smooth one.

Without warning, he flipped her. Poised on top and clasping her wrists in his grip. "Gotcha."

Laughing, Connie wriggled, but couldn't escape. Not that she wanted to. "Tough guy!"

"Like I said—gotcha." When he bent to take a nipple between his lips, excitement rolled over her in waves.

She loved the sense of being held within his power, cherished and commanded as he loomed over her. This was a different Hale, a man who instinctively understood her and made no apology for indulging.

The pressure of his renewed penetration made her gasp. He released her wrists to brace himself as he caught fire. Faster and faster…she'd never flown so close to the sun. Inside Connie, flames seared away old scar tissue and she felt born anew in Hale's embrace.

As shudders ran through him, she heard a kind of sob, not of sorrow but of joy. They sank into the sheets, sweaty and spent. For a long moment Connie doubted her ability to stir. Then she felt Hale scuffling beneath the covers as he disposed of their protection. She hoped they had another, or two or three. Enough to last all night.

After they made love for the second time, Hale drifted gradually down from a state of bliss. Couldn't believe this had happened or how transcendent it felt. The qualities that had always both fascinated and tormented him—Connie's intelligence, her zest, her sharp edges—had elevated their merging into the realm of the extraordinary.

The other women Hale had dated faded to distant memories. While he'd liked and respected them, something had always been lacking in their involvement.

Connie seemed intensely real to him in a way that made Hale long to create a safe haven where she and Skip could flourish. To see her smile each morning and sleep in her arms each night.

If only relationships were that simple.

He shifted onto his side, careful not to dislodge the woman sleeping beside him. How precious she looked, hair in a tangle, smooth legs brushing his calves. If only he could believe that, fundamentally, things had changed. Yet Hale had no doubt he would continue to irritate her almost beyond endurance and that her nit-picking might drive him to drink. Well, to toss down a couple of beers with the guys, anyway.

And there'd be hell to pay when Joel found out. Hale's father wasn't going to react well, either. On a weekend visit to Dad's cabin during the divorce proceedings, Joel had painted Connie as shallow, selfish and fickle. Mack Crandall, who already held a grudge against the female gender thanks to his wife's abandonment, wasn't likely to cut her any slack.

Well, Hale had always lived full-out. No holds barred. He'd wanted Connie and now, apparently, he had a chance with her.

He meant to do his best to make this work.

Chapter Thirteen

For Connie, the weekend sped by too fast. On Sunday, Hale gave Skip another swimming lesson, to the child's delight, and promised another the following weekend. On Sunday night, the two of them made love again, but Hale didn't sleep over, since both had to be at work the following day. Thank goodness none of their friends dropped by, because anyone seeing them would have immediately grasped that they'd become lovers.

At the shop Monday, Connie learned to her relief that Sunday's sales had proceeded normally. So far, the harassment hadn't seriously affected business, but she believed in aggressive retailing. If she tried to coast, sooner or later Joel or a rival shop or changing public tastes would send Connie's Curios the way of dozens of other failed retail operations.

She filled the area formerly devoted to candy with an array of miniature furry creatures, but considered that a mere stopgap. Prime space deserved a more productive use, so, one afternoon in midweek, she agreed to meet with local entrepreneur Zandy Watts, who custom-made novelties, clothing and accessories.

"Unique products, say, your own line of handbags, reinforce customer loyalty and boost sales," the woman said as they sat in Connie's cramped office. In her forties with cropped salt-and-pepper hair, the large-boned Zandy seemed almost too dynamic for the small space. Connie kept one ear attuned to sounds from the shop. Although she had confidence in the new clerk, she feared Joel would pull another stunt.

"I like your designs," she said, flipping through a catalog. She had been searching for a way to expand sales on her website and to draw customers from a wider geographic region. A line of unique products might do the trick—but it would have to be eye-catching and special. "We'd need an approach with attitude."

They spent the next hour brainstorming. Instead of simply using variations of products already in Zandy's catalog, Connie visualized a line combining down-to-earth fabrics such as denim and canvas with lacy or flowered inserts and trim. "Maybe matching outfits for little girls and their moms," she said. "And boy stuff, too—without the lace and flowers, of course. Parent-and-child baseball caps, for instance."

"Fabulous!"

A possible title occurred to Connie. "What about Con Amore? That's Italian for 'with love.' And it reflects my name, too."

Zandy stared at her, then let out a whoop. "That's perfect! Catchy and instantly memorable! We've got good chemistry and I like your style, Connie. Want to consider a joint venture—a limited partnership?"

Connie nearly forgot to breathe. She'd dreamed of trying a large-scale adventure, but hadn't expected to stumble across an opportunity so soon.

Still, she had to be practical. "I can't spare much capital."

"You already operate retail sites and I have

manufacturing capability," Zandy noted. "There'll be start-up costs and materials, but that shouldn't be onerous. I'll crunch the numbers."

"We'll require a business plan and of course a contract between us." Fortunately, Connie had already arranged for a modest line of credit against her house in case of emergency. She hadn't tapped it yet, but this might be worth the risk. "Definitely, let's pursue this."

They made another appointment for the following week. When they shook hands, Connie got the feeling they were at the start of a major undertaking. Amazing that the key aspects of her life were surging forward simultaneously. A child, a man and a business expansion. Amazing!

Six o'clock already, she discovered. Brimming with inspiration, she sent her clerk home, then hurried to lock up the shop. When she stepped outside, however, renewed concern about what else Joel might try twisted through her.

The parking lot appeared normal, however. And Detective Tenille had called that afternoon with the good news that the medical examination disclosed no foreign substances in Skip's stomach. Apparently the candy bar switching had been more of a prank than an assault. The downside was that, as a result, state and federal authorities appeared unlikely to intervene. The local investigation remained open, although Vince had been provisionally cleared. He had an alibi for Saturday, when he'd spent the afternoon helping Yolanda make repairs at the fourplex.

Since Paris hadn't been able to identify Joel from a photo lineup, he, too, might escape repercussions. Connie wasn't sure what she wished would happen to him. Losing his job or going to jail seemed excessive, yet she seethed with resentment at the way Skip had suffered.

She glanced up, distracted, as a blue van rumbled past. Blinking against a flash of sunlight, she frowned at a fragment of memory. Had she seen it here on Saturday?

The vehicle swung around a line of parked cars too quickly for her to catch any details. She got the impression it bore out-of-state license plates, but perhaps she'd failed to recognize one of California's special fund-raising editions.

In her purse, the phone rang. When she answered, Hale said, “How about I pick up fried chicken and we picnic on my patio?”

“Great plan.” In the joy of hearing his voice, Connie dismissed the blue van. “I’m just leaving to get Skip.”

“See you shortly.”

“You bet.”

She cradled the phone in her palm, warmed by the contact. On the surface of their interaction, so little had changed since last weekend. Yet at a deeper level, tectonic plates were shifting. She only hoped that when the continents came to rest, she and Hale still stood on the same one.

On Saturday morning, Hale took a leisurely shower at Connie’s after breakfast. He really should have gone home, since he’d have to change into his swim trunks before the planned lesson, anyway, but he liked the delicate scent of her bathroom and the thickness of her towels. Ought to find out where she bought them and purchase a set of his own, he mused.

Hale meandered out of the steamy chamber, fully dressed but barefoot, wet hair slicked back. From the den, one of Skip’s favorite cartoons blared from the TV. Closer at hand, he caught the rasp of tense voices—a couple of seconds too late, because by then he'd wandered within full view of the living room.

And Joel. The open door indicated he must have arrived only moments earlier.

Hale halted as his friend's jaw snapped shut. "Greetings," Hale said affably.

He'd never realized that a guy could look angry down to the roots of his hair, but Joel definitely had angry hair. Also narrowed eyes and hands that formed nasty-looking fists.

"I can see whose side *you're* on, *buddy,*" Joel said.

"I'm not on anybody's side," Hale responded instinctively. "I mean..." He shot Connie a look.

Mercifully, she picked up the conversational ball. "Joel dropped by to plead his case." Hands on hips, she stood rigidly in the center of the room like a watchdog guarding its territory. Well, a very feminine watchdog wearing a flimsy bathrobe that emphasized her curves. "If I understand correctly, he believes I'm on a vendetta and that if I'd only back off like a good little girl, the PD would drop the matter."

"Confronting your ex-wife is a bad idea."

His friend ought to be aware that this sort of behavior would count against him.

"Don't try to order me around!" the man exploded. "Especially under the circumstances!"

Great. Next thing they'd be duking it out in Connie's living room and terrifying Skip. Hale raised his hands in a *halt* gesture. "If you came to talk, don't let me stop you."

Connie sat on the arm of the sofa, skepticism written across her face. "I'm dying to hear the rest of this, Joel."

Her ex made a gesture of frustration. "You know perfectly well I wouldn't substitute bars with nuts in them. My sister's allergic."

A shadow—doubt?—crossed Connie's face. She used to work at a furniture store with Joel's sister Bonnie, Hale recalled. In fact, Bonnie had introduced the pair.

"She may have mentioned it," Connie acknowledged.

"She nearly died when she was in junior high!" Joel snapped. "I'd never risk doing that to anyone else."

"The incident happened nearly twenty years ago. But okay, how do you explain the business card?"

Under examination, it had revealed several fingerprints smeared beyond recognition, and one identifiable as Joel's. Regardless of who had dropped it, at least the card wasn't a fake.

"Okay, it must be mine. But that doesn't prove I was in your store!" he declared.

"It doesn't prove you weren't, either," Connie retorted.

Hale had to admit the evidence *did* appear to point to Joel. But Connie ought to realize that the man's weaknesses—being impulsive and blunt—didn't jibe with the sneaky behavior of her tormenter. Nor did Hale consider Joel capable of standing here in front of them both and lying persuasively.

"I've been trying to remember who I've given cards to recently. I don't use them a lot." Joel leaned against a frail table, which shifted beneath his weight. He instinctively grabbed it, then glanced at the bare surface in confusion. "What happened to the froufrou crap you used to put everywhere?"

"I childproofed," Connie said tersely.

"You mean you're capable of change?"

This argument poised on the brink of mudslinging, Hale feared. "Let's stick to the subject."

His old pal rewarded him with a glower. "She refused to clear that garbage for me!"

"That's because you aren't six years old, even if you act like it," his ex-wife sniped.

As Hale had foreseen, the discussion was disintegrating. "Your business cards," he reminded Joel. "Who'd you give them to?"

The visitor grimaced. "A businessman I had to calm down when he didn't like the way the desk officer handled his complaint. A lady from the chamber of commerce that Derek was giving a tour of the station. And a couple of weeks ago I slipped one to a waitress at Jose's Tavern after we flirted. Never heard from her again."

Connie bit her lip. Probably suppressing a snide remark.

"Did you tell Kirk about them?" Hale asked.

"Yeah, he located the first two. They still had the cards. He can't find the waitress. Apparently she quit."

The temptation overwhelmed Connie's restraint. "Too many cops hitting on her?"

Joel smacked his fist into his palm. "Waste of effort coming here. Stupid of me to think I could reason with a vindictive witch."

Hale refused to stand by for insults. "You're way out of bounds, bud."

"Out of bounds?" Connie said. "He's out

of control!" Anger propelled her forward, closer to her ex. "I'll tell you what's going on. You still believe you have the right to run my life. You resented my opening the stores, you hate that I'm making a success of them and you're furious because I'm adopting a child. So you're doing your best to screw everything up!"

"I haven't done a blessed thing to you," Joel shot back, towering over her. "I'll bet you ticked off some other guy and won't admit it."

"Is that how you rationalize your criminal behavior? That I somehow *deserve* it?" She stopped, peering past him out the door. "Who's that?"

Hale hoped the arrival of a gardener or deliveryman might cut short the fruitless squabble. Instead, heavy footsteps on the porch yielded to the unexpected sight of Hale's father.

Mack Crandall's heavy-lidded gaze swept the three of them. "Interrupting something?" he asked. "Sorry to intrude but nobody answered the bell next door."

"What brings you to town, Dad?"

"Just visiting." Although Tahoe lay a full day's drive away, Mack occasionally paid an unannounced visit to see old friends and hang out in his former stomping grounds. He seemed to consider advance warning an unnecessary frill.

Usually, his son was glad to see him. But not today, when he had plans with Connie.

Hale hid his dismay behind a show of politeness as he launched into an introduction. If the stars were aligned properly, maybe he could quickly steer his visitor across the property line and out of harm's way.

But he wasn't keen on the odds.

Connie bristled as the older man's gaze swept her. He appeared to be leering.

"I was just on my way out," Joel said, evidently deciding the better of continuing to spar with her.

"What's your hurry?" Mack slapped him on the arm. "Let's go target shooting, the three of us."

"I have plans this morning," Hale countered.

Good for him, Connie thought. He wasn't going to bail out on Skip's swim lesson.

"With this little gal?" Mack remarked. "I sure like the way she dresses." This time, there was no mistaking the lewdness in his gaze.

Annoyed, Connie pulled her flimsy bathrobe tighter. "It *happens* to be Saturday morning and a couple of people *happened* to drop into my house uninvited."

"What did I say?" the man asked blandly.

"Knock it off, Dad." Hale folded his arms.

Mack radiated pretend innocence. "Hey, a fellow has eyes, doesn't he? Anyway, I'm only staying for the weekend. I should think my only child could spare me one day."

Skip, still in his pjs, poked his nose out of the hall. "What child?"

Mack frowned. "Who're you?"

"That's my son, Skip," Connie interceded.

"He's my swimming student," Hale added. "We have a lesson this morning."

"I'm sure the little guy will understand if a man shows some respect for his father," Mack said. "Won't you, fella?"

Skip stared at him in confusion. "I s'pose."

"What do you expect him to say?" Connie snapped. "You guys obviously like to push people around."

"Nobody's pushing you around," Joel groused.

"I wonder why you find male bonding so threatening," Mack joined in.

Hale needed to clear these two off the premises, now. "Lay off her. Both of you."

"Don't fight!" Skip wailed.

Connie's heart contracted. "We aren't fighting, sweetheart. Just...disagreeing."

Hale hunkered down to the boy's level. "Is it okay if we postpone our swim lesson until tomorrow? It'll be extra long, I promise."

Skip's lower lip trembled. "Okay."

"You sure?"

The little boy hugged him. "Mmm-hmm," he murmured into Hale's collar.

Although Connie realized Mack Crandall had put his son in an awkward position, she still wished Hale had stood up to him, for Skip's sake. For hers, too.

"We'd better go before the range gets crowded," Mack said. "I'll treat you boys to lunch, too. You'll join us, won't you, Joel?"

"Yeah, sure. Thanks," he muttered.

Skip frowned. "They aren't boys."

Connie responded more for the benefit of her uninvited guests than for her son. "Maturity has nothing to do with the passage of years, honey. You've already got better manners than a lot of grown-ups." Addressing them directly, she said, "Now why don't you *boys* go play with your guns?"

Joel ducked out, clearly in a foul mood.

Mack's jaw moved, but his irritation subsided when Hale shot him a warning glance.

After his father stepped outside, Hale spoke softly to Connie. "I'm sorry. I think it's best to avoid a scene in front of Skip, and my father's set in his ways. I try to humor him."

"Fine. Have fun." She couldn't blame Hale, but how could she not feel disappointed?

After retrieving his wallet and repeating his assurances to Skip about tomorrow, he departed. Watching the three men through the window, the little boy formed a picture of dejection.

"He'll tell me a story tonight, won't he?" he asked.

"I expect so." Connie looked forward to Hale's nightly visits, too. "I've got an idea! Go get dressed and grab your bathing suit."

While Skip raced off to dress, she dialed her mother, who lived twenty miles away in Coto de Caza. The expansive house with its rarely used pool had been part of the settlement from her mom's second marriage. It represented a complete change from the condominium in Villazon where Connie had grown up. In those days, Anna—a former actress whose career had fizzled after a few small roles on television—had held a job as a receptionist in an insurance office.

"Fabulous! I can't wait to meet my grandson!" Anna injected total sincerity into the claim, although until now she'd declined invitations to drive to Villazon. "Please join me for lunch."

"Thanks, Mom." Connie refrained from suggesting that Skip might prefer something heartier than the light salads her mother usually served. They could always stop by a restaurant later.

Less than an hour later, she found herself lounging beside a pool at the Mediterranean-style villa while Skip cavorted in the shallow end of the pool. The still-glamorous Anna, who kept fit by swimming each morning, showed no inclination to play with her grandson. Instead, she perched on a chaise beside Connie, painting her toenails fiery red with sparkles. Her platinum hair, longer and thicker than her daughter's thanks to the talents of a top-notch stylist, draped youthfully around her shoulders.

"What did you expect from a friend of Joel's?" she inquired after Connie related the story. "Honey, I don't know what you see in these cops."

"Hale's sexy," Connie confided. "And handy around the house."

"Marry a man with money and hire someone else to do the chores."

Connie supposed her life would be easier if she were attracted to wealthy executive types. A big house, designer clothing, servants...but also a sense that she'd been bought and paid for. No, thanks.

After capping the polish bottle, Anna swished a hand above her toenails to speed the drying. "You ought to sell this type of polish at your store. It's a specialty brand you can only buy at salons."

"There's a nail salon next to us. They carry beautiful stuff." Soraya's Nails had been established since Anna's last visit to Connie's Curios, more than a year ago. "But let me tell you about this new idea!"

She sketched the notion of the Con Amore line. Her mother loved it, and joined in with relish. "How about Con Amore Wearables and Bearables?" she proposed.

"Bearables?"

"Things you carry—purses, totes and umbrellas," Anna explained. "Plus the word *bearables* will let you incorporate teddy bears into the designs. I suppose they're overused, but with a good designer you can make them your own, and they're always appealing."

"I like that," Connie said. "I'll run it by Zandy."

A short time later, Anna's housekeeper served their meal by the pool. Along with tuna salads, she'd prepared nachos and fruit salad for Skip. Afterward, Connie bid her mother farewell and drove up the coast to Newport Beach, where she and her son strolled around the harbor's edge admiring the sailboats.

Although they had fun, she missed Hale's wry observations and suspected Skip would have treasured his company. But she was grateful for the little hand in hers and for the simple pleasure of eating ice-cream cones together. And besides, they'd see him tonight. The humorous tales of Hale's childhood antics had become a sacred ritual.

Her phone rang as they headed toward her car. She guessed the purpose as soon as she heard Hale's apologetic voice.

"I'm sorry, but I have to beg off for tonight." From the background echoed the crash of bowling pins. "A couple of Dad's old chums joined us for bowling. One of them invited us to a pre-Fourth of July barbecue. A lot of folks we used to know will be there."

"Can't miss that." Despite her words, Connie's spirits sank.

"I'd invite you and Skip, but I doubt you'd choose to be anywhere near Dad and Joel," he added.

She sighed. "You're right about that."

"We're still on for tomorrow, though. Okay?"

"Absolutely." Connie didn't intend to let hurt feelings get in the way of their relationship. Except that, as she clicked off, she wondered how much of a relationship she could count on.

She crouched and explained the situation. Rather than admit that Hale had canceled their plans to attend a party, she mentioned his obligation to his father. "Mack will be gone tomorrow and we'll have Hale to ourselves again."

"He's lucky to have a real dad," Skip said sadly. "I wish I did."

"He sure is." A lump formed in her chest. "I don't feel like going home yet, do you?"

"No," he agreed.

"Let's drive to the beach." It lay on the opposite side of the narrow peninsula. Parking might be tricky at this hour of the afternoon, but with luck they'd find a space. "You can play and we'll buy dinner at one of the eateries along the strand."

"Okay." Obediently, Skip climbed into the car.

Connie fastened the belt over his booster seat. "At least you've got me. And you always will."

He patted her arm. "I love you, Mommy."

An unexpected shot of happiness quivered through Connie. He'd not only called her Mommy, he'd said the words she longed most to hear.

"I love you, too. Heaps and bundles." Tears misted her eyes.

Despite the setback with Hale, today had yielded a small miracle. Her heart much lighter, Connie put the car into gear and set out for the beach.

Fried clams and onion rings, served with a side of sand and a full measure of love. No barbecue on earth could compete with that.

Chapter Fourteen

Hale didn't much like the man he saw in the mirror on Sunday morning. The bleary eyes and the unshaven jaw were bad enough, but beneath them lurked the fellow who'd disappointed a little boy—and the woman he cared about.

The fellow in the glass enjoyed having his cake and eating it, too. He expected to remain one of the boys while assuming the role of boyfriend and big brother. Well, today he meant to honor his promise to Skip and make amends with Connie, as well.

Could he actually get away with leading a life on two planes? Hale wondered. He was bound to pay a price. His lonely bed this morning and his dissatisfaction with his behavior demonstrated the truth of that.

A hot shower, a couple of toaster pastries and two cups of coffee helped restore his innate optimism. He was outside unrolling the pool cover when Connie peered over the wall.

"Morning, Hale," she said. "I have a favor to ask. If you don't mind."

"You mean I might escape a scolding?" he teased.

She appeared somewhat disconcerted. "I guess we're both doing our best to cope with a complicated world," she conceded.

Hale was happy to accept a truce. "I'm glad we're still on good terms. What's the favor?"

"One of my clerks is sick today and the other one's too new to run the place alone." She consulted her watch. "It's eleven already and we open at noon. Would you be willing to...?"

"Mind Skip? No problem." Having unveiled the pool, he keyed open the gate. "Where's our little man?"

"Catching the end of a show. He'll be out in a minute." She lingered, a study in mixed emotions.

Hale prowled through the gap in the wall.

When he reached for her, Connie hesitated, and then she slid right into his arms for a long, passionate kiss.

Reluctantly, they separated. As they did, he remembered he hadn't finished setting the record straight. "I apologize for my father. He's…old-fashioned toward women in the worst sense."

"I'm glad it didn't rub off on his son." Connie's smile warmed Hale.

"Was Skip upset?"

"A little," she answered, "but we swam at my mom's house and played on the beach. Skip was so worn out, he couldn't have stayed awake for a story, anyway."

"So he didn't miss me?"

She brushed out her ruffled red skirt. What a vivid picture it made against her blue-and-white blouse. "Actually, he did."

Now he felt bad again. "Does he understand why I had to accommodate my father?"

"Yes. He…" Connie pressed her lips into a line.

Hale traced a finger down her cheek. Soft skin and a smooth complexion, with just a hint of a tan. "The suspense is killing me."

"Honestly, it wasn't important."

He interpreted that to mean the opposite.

"Persistence is the hallmark of a good detective. Might as well spill it now."

She yielded. "He said you were lucky to have a real dad."

A real dad. As opposed to a fake one? Or rather, as opposed to the kind who popped in for brief sessions and disappeared when he found a little boy inconvenient. The insight was troubling. The role of big brother no longer entirely satisfied him, he supposed. This business of having his cake and eating it too was already proving awkward.

Connie continued talking, apparently unaware of his conflicting emotions. "Here's the terrific part. He called me Mommy and said, 'I love you.' I didn't expect that so soon! I was a little afraid it might not happen at all."

Hale felt pleased for her sake, but also oddly deflated. "Congratulations. That's quite a breakthrough and you deserve it."

Connie's back door opened and a small figure emerged clutching an armload of gear. Skinny body sporting swim trunks and flip-flops, Skip navigated the yard. A few weeks ago, Hale hadn't known this kid from any youngster on the street. Now the little guy filled a special niche in his heart.

A question occurred to him. "What's his real name?"

"Edward." Connie reached to ruffle the boy's hair, then said to her son, "Hale says it's okay to spend the day with him."

"Yippee!" Joy transformed his solemn expression. "All day?"

"'Til dinner at least," Hale assured him. Edward, huh? A name suitable for the years ahead, when the little frame grew tall and sturdy.

"I'll be good, I promise." Skip gazed up at him. "I won't get in your way. I'll sit in a corner and be real quiet."

"Oh, really?" Hale feigned regret. "I planned for us to play in the pool this morning and go to a movie after lunch. Don't you want to?"

"Yes!" Eagerness and uncertainty warred in the boy's eyes.

Hale knelt to face him. "Listen, pardner, I'm sorry I let you down yesterday. But today's going to be different. And you're no trouble, believe me." He added teasingly, "I might even have a few peanut butter cookies in the pantry for lunch."

"Healthy meals," Connie warned.

Skip scowled. "Mo-om!"

"Of course you can eat cookies," she said gently, "but good nutrition is important."

As Skip screwed up his face to protest, Hale intervened. "It's a mom's job to keep you healthy. You're lucky she loves you enough to play food police for your own good. So we'll eat a healthy lunch and *then* we'll have cookies."

"Okay." After giving him mother a quick kiss, the boy hauled his gear through the gate.

"You handled that well," Connie told him. "Thanks for not undercutting me just to score points with him."

"That's the last thing I'd do."

She laid one hand on his arm. "That is one of the big differences between you and Joel. He cut me down every chance he got. Well, I'll see you at six."

Hale watched her retrace her steps, red skirt swishing. Her last comment reverberated in his mind. He'd heard Joel's side of their breakup for so long that he hadn't noticed how skewed it was. Hale had been so aware of Joel's undeserved hassles at the department and his need for his wife's sympathy that his friend's rough-hewn behavior and negative comments about her had all slid under the radar.

A playful shout from Skip cut off the reminiscing. Hale hurried to join the boy in the pool.

Today's progress included actual swimming along with a couple of feet-first plunges off the edge. Hale took care not to push too hard, however. When the boy wearied of the activity, Hale provided him with the remote-control boat and retreated to a nearby lounger with a paperback thriller. He had trouble focusing on the story, however. Too much stuff to think about.

Yesterday, he'd asked Joel a question that had troubled him since the incident with the candy. Why *had* he declined an invitation to the movies that day? He'd produced no alibi other than a vague comment about strolling in Mesa View Park, a patch of green south of city hall. With a duck pond and playground, it was far from a hot spot for bachelors.

"I had this urge to hang around families," Joel had admitted as they flipped burgers and hot dogs at last night's barbecue. "Observe how they handle their kids and absorb the vibes."

"Tell me this isn't a weird new hobby," Hale had said.

"That little boy Connie's adopting brought me up short," Joel had answered. "When I insisted we have a baby, I wasn't dealing with reality. I had the naive idea a baby would fix our marriage." Joel had snared a blackened wiener from the grill, blown on it and downed a bite. "Don't you dare tell my ex, but in retrospect, I wasn't ready to be a parent. "

"So this walk in the park meant—?"

"I've been feeling an urge to be a father. Half hoped the sight of real kids would drive it out of me, but no such luck. Maybe one of these days I'll meet the right lady."

"So you're not picturing Connie in this role?" Hale needed to be sure. He hated the vague feelings of guilt that still plagued him.

"Are you kidding?" Joel took another bite. "No way. She's all yours. Living next door, and her being so good-looking, I can't exactly blame you."

Hale had learned that Kirk's investigation was zeroing in on Joel, but the notion that this man had tampered with food and risked injuring a child seemed outrageous.

Across the patio, Skip chattered merrily as he steered the boat. Someone had forced that little guy to endure a miserable evening of harsh tests, and put Connie through the wringer. Not Joel. But someone who might get away with it.

Hale couldn't let that happen. Unfortunately, this case was officially none of his business.

All week the media had hounded Chief Lyons about the fire and the food tampering, insinuating a cover-up to protect his son in the first incident and complaining that no suspect had been apprehended in the other. The result: pressure to wrap up the cases fast and present them to the D.A.

Hale couldn't do much for Ben Lyons, but he might be able to aid Joel by speaking up. He disliked ruffling feathers and hated controversies, but at least he could point out to the powers-that-be how easily a rush to judgment might backfire.

He'd better do it fast, regardless of whose toes he stepped on in the short run. Even if they belonged to Connie. Ultimately, the only way to protect her was to identify the real perp and, whether or not anyone else agreed, Hale was becoming more and more convinced that wouldn't turn out to be Joel.

"I hope they never let you work undercover, because you're the worst person in the world at hiding your feelings," Connie told Hale as they cuddled in her den that evening.

After a lengthy good-night story that in her opinion more than compensated for last night's absence, they'd tucked Skip into bed half an hour earlier. Suffused with goodwill after seeing her son's contentment, she'd practically tackled Hale on the sofa. But her enthusiasm had faded when she realized he was holding back.

"I have a few things on my mind," he conceded, plopping his sock-clad feet onto the coffee table.

"Care to share?"

His words escaped in a rush. "The bureau's railroading Joel. I can't let that happen."

Connie almost wished she hadn't asked. "You're not the detective on the case." She rested her cheek on his shoulder. *Leave this alone. Don't let Joel come between us.*

"Politics and public relations shouldn't influence this investigation, but that's what's happening," he responded gravely. "I have to do what's right."

Reluctantly, she drew back. "And what *is* right? Sticking by your friend no matter who he hurts?"

"If I believed he was behind this…"

"What would it take to convince you?" To her dismay, she heard a tremor in her voice. "Hale, when he barged into the house yesterday morning, he scared me. I was so grateful you were here."

"I agree, he shouldn't have come." Hale addressed the wall. "I believe he's innocent, which means somebody else is guilty. I want that person caught."

Connie wished he'd meet her gaze. "You're choosing him over me."

"I'm choosing you both!" Again, he addressed the wall.

She couldn't stand to see Hale deceive himself. "I respect your role as a peacemaker. That's the way you grew up, running interference for your dad, and that's obviously one of the qualities your fellow officers appreciate about you. So do I. But this time you can't have it both ways!" She halted, aching to shake the delusions out of him.

He exhaled slowly and finally turned to face her. "You're very precious to me, Connie. But I can't substitute another person's judgment for my own. Not even yours."

They'd reached the point she'd dreaded from the moment she began letting Hale close, the point at which he had to decide where his loyalties lay. And he was choosing his buddies. Not only Joel but the whole male pack, his father included. He had so much to offer a family, but without full and unqualified commitment, he'd only break her heart and her son's, as well.

She'd spent most of her teen years yearning for her father's approval, sending him wish-you-were-here cards and photos of the big events in her life, seeking a response that never came. Granted, Hale showed a lot more warmth and tenderness toward Skip than Jim Lawson ever had to her. But then, her marriage to Joel had started off promisingly, too. Joel had bought her the wedding ring of her dreams, a blue-white diamond set in a swirl of emeralds. He'd claimed it symbolized how much she meant to him. Now she could scarcely bear to look at the thing.

Connie had begun to hope that, with Hale, she'd found a guy who not only loved her but could offer the partnership she needed. Instead, he'd buckled under pressure from his pal. Unless she could trust him one hundred percent, she didn't dare risk continuing this relationship. Especially not with a child in the picture.

"I'm sorry," she whispered. "I thought we…" She couldn't complete the sentence.

"Me, too," Hale replied so gently that she ached. "I hope you'll see things differently when this is finished."

"I'm afraid it's finished already." Connie stared down at her hands. "Between us, I mean."

He didn't answer, simply sat there for a minute, then stood up and left, limping a little. The recognition of his vulnerability nearly brought a burst of tears.

She'd sent him away. For Skip's sake, perhaps they should continue with the story times, but that was all. She'd rather end on a quietly regretful note than drag this on until they parted with bitterness.

Feeling miserable, Connie turned off the lights, set the alarm and went to bed. Alone.

On Monday morning, Hale watched for an opportunity to express his concerns. And to whom—for his immediate superior, Lieutenant E. J. Corwin, had stayed home with a badly bruised hip from an ill-advised spin on his son's motorbike. When Kirk Tenille's phone rang and at the same moment Captain Frank Ferguson emerged from his office, both apparently summoned to the chief's office, Hale stood up and followed. Might get thrown out on his ear, but what the heck.

Lois Lamont raised an eyebrow as he trailed the others past her desk, but said nothing. And neither Chief Lyons nor Ferguson objected when Hale stepped into the large, sunny room. Each probably believed the other had requested his presence, he realized with a tickle of amusement.

He eased into a chair and held his peace while Kirk ran through the evidence against Joel. The business card on the floor bearing Joel's name. The threat he'd issued to Connie, his unconfirmed location on Saturday and the unverifiable story about handing a card to a waitress who'd apparently quit in a huff and left no forwarding address. Yolanda Rios confirming the alibi of the only other suspect, Vince Borrego.

"This is all we've got so far, Chief," Frank remarked when Tenille finished. "I'd hardly call it conclusive."

Hale prayed they'd simply continue to investigate instead of handing the case to the D.A. Then he wouldn't have to say anything.

"The perp already sent a little boy to the hospital, and we're possibly dealing with a vengeful ex-husband," Lyons said tautly. "What if he turns violent and we did nothing to stop him?"

"Mrs. Simmons could obtain a restraining order," Kirk ventured.

"Lot of good that would do," Hale muttered before realizing he was undercutting his purpose. "Okay, I'm not keen on the effectiveness of restraining orders, but also I have my doubts about Joel's guilt. Did he tell you that his sister nearly died of a nut allergy? He wouldn't pull a stunt like that lightly."

"Harassing one's ex-wife isn't a course anyone pursues lightly," Lyons responded.

"Okay. Here's another concern." Hale leaned forward. "I'm convinced the perp is someone else. Someone smart enough to frame Joel, which means that once you go to the D.A., he's probably also smart enough to lie low. And don't forget the man Mrs. Rios spotted before the fire. He may have planted a lit marijuana cigarette in your son's couch." Hale's newfound forcefulness had silenced his listeners. "Both matters are an embarrassment to this department. So that's another possible motive."

The chief nodded slowly. "We can't hold off long. What do you propose?"

Hale thought fast. "I'll pay another visit to the tavern and see what I can learn regarding the waitress. If that's the only one of Joel's cards unaccounted for, it's worth pursuing."

Tenille spoke defensively. "The owner says she left the area."

Judging by the report, efforts to find the woman had been perfunctory. The detective's laxness annoyed Hale. "Did you consider that if there *is* a conspiracy against this department and she *did* provide the card, she might have suffered harm, or left for her own protection?"

The younger man swallowed hard without answering. Obviously that angle hadn't occurred to him.

"The mayor's scheduled a press conference at two this afternoon to update the media," Lyons said. "He's asked us to at least provide a preliminary conclusion."

Oh, great, Hale thought. The powers-that-be had set a deadline to sacrifice an innocent man. "I'll get right on it." With that, he strode out. Lois, who must have overheard, gave him a thumbs-up. He smiled.

Hale could scarcely believed he'd dominated a meeting he'd had no business attending. If the chief and the captain respected him that much, he'd missed a good bet by dodging his chances at promotion. On the other hand, maybe he'd just blown those chances. But there was a lot more at stake here than his personal ambitions.

As he grabbed his briefcase, Hale wondered if Jose's Tavern was open yet—it was only midmorning. After his performance in front of the chief and the captain, he didn't dare return empty-handed.

Chapter Fifteen

Connie took Skip with her to work that morning, since she needed to drive him to an appointment with Dr. Federov. It was the first visit he'd paid to the shop since the chocolate bar incident, and he clung to her for the first few minutes. After that, however, he settled down in the office with a coloring book.

Zandy called, bubbling over with excitement at the numbers she'd come up with for Con Amore. "I can hardly wait to see you! How about this afternoon?"

Despite her enthusiasm, Connie wasn't prepared to meet so soon. "I'd like more time to research. Let's wait 'til Thursday as we planned."

"Okay. Guess I'm a little carried away, but this is *so* exciting! The figures are lower than I'd expected."

"And I've got tons of ideas about products. We'll go over them Thursday."

As she hung up, Connie realized that lack of preparation wasn't her only reason for postponing. Today, she felt off her game.

"You okay?" inquired Jo Anne, who'd just finished checking out a customer with an armload of Fourth of July gear.

"I'm a little down, I guess. Hale and I reached a parting of the ways. Except as friends, of course." Connie had tossed and turned all night, alternately missing him and itching to ring him up and talk.

"Hey, you can't expect to hit a home run the first time you get your feet wet after a divorce," commiserated her assistant. Connie had confided in her about the affair.

"Mom, mixed metaphor!" Paris called from where she stood arranging a display of sun visors. "Who plays baseball in a wading pool?"

"Kids!" her mother declared. "Always nitpicking!"

Despite her mood, Connie chuckled. "You guys are hilarious."

"By the way," Jo Anne said, "shouldn't the seniors' bus be here by now?"

The Palm Street Assisted Living Center provided its residents with biweekly shopping tours that included Connie's Curios. In appreciation, the store gave a discount to participants.

"They don't always operate on schedule. But you're right. They *are* a little late. And so am I!" Connie should have left for Skip's appointment five minutes ago. "Gotta rush."

Skip trotted beside Connie to the car, keen to see the psychologist again. Despite the cost of the sessions, they were paying off. Her relationship with Skip had improved immeasurably, and his nightmares had virtually ceased. Connie intended to consult the doctor periodically as her son grew.

She was switching on the ignition when a blue vehicle showed in her rearview mirror. Connie waited for it to pass before backing out. When she did and saw the vehicle now at the end of the aisle, she realized it was a blue van bearing out-of-state plates she couldn't immediately identify. The sight of it bothered her.

"Big sky," Skip announced.

"What?" she asked distractedly.

"That's what it says on the van." He spoke proudly.

"Good for you! You read the license plates." Mentally, Connie tried to place the motto. Big Sky State. Montana, she recalled.

Out-of-state vehicles weren't unusual in California. Nothing suspicious about that. She noted, however, how the van slowed as it neared the front of her shop. Was the driver looking for someone or something?

An all-but-forgotten glimmer of memory returned unexpectedly. She hadn't merely seen the van the Saturday of the food tampering, she'd waited for it to vacate a space when she and Skip arrived. If the driver was a Connie's Curios customer, he or she might have entered the premises about the same time as whoever substituted the candy bars. Possibly a witness who could identify Joel!

Or could Joel have borrowed the van from a friend? That would certainly have helped cover his tracks.

Just as Connie prepared to swing by and copy the license number, however, the Palm Street Center courtesy bus approached from the opposite direction. As if in response, the van sped out of the parking lot onto the adjacent street, too fast for her to catch up.

A sense of frustration persisted as she drove to Dr. Federov's office. Was she wrong in attaching some significance to the van?

At the psychologist's, the receptionist reminded her that this was a solo meeting with Skip, which gave her a free hour. Connie decided to cross the street to the precinct and tell Hale what she'd observed. She didn't want to delude herself that winding up the case would mend the differences between them. But she looked forward to seeing him all the same.

Jose's Tavern wasn't due to open for another fifteen minutes. But when Hale rapped hard on the door, he caught sight of movement through the dark glass. He held up his badge and pointed at it.

A bolt snicked aside. He recognized the sturdy woman who opened it as the bartender who'd waited on him and Joel. "What's up, Officer?"

He obtained her name—Katherine Ayle, although she urged him to address her as Kat—and explained that he was investigating a series of incidents possibly related to a stalking. "I need to question a waitress who used to work here—Laura Niven."

"She quit without notice. Didn't leave an

address." Kat glanced toward the interior of the tavern.

"Someone else on the premises?" Hale inquired.

She rolled her eyes. "The owner. He's always lurking."

Her tone indicated an inability to speak freely. "Let's step outside."

Kat joined him on the walkway and shut the door. "He'll stick his nose out any second."

"What is it you don't want him to hear?"

A large truck passed on the street, its grinding gears drowning their voices. When the noise abated, Kat replied, "Laura quit because that jerk kept pestering her for dates, even threatened her. I urged her to report him, but she preferred to quit."

"So she didn't move out of the area?"

"Heck, no. That's just what she told *him*." Kat glanced toward the window. "She changed her phone number and vacated her apartment, but she's staying with her parents in the Amber View development. I don't know the street number, but it's a beige house with turquoise trim at the corner of Willow and Cypress."

He jotted down the description. "Did she mention a police officer giving her a business card?"

"No, like I told the other detective. Is it important?"

"Perhaps." He wasn't about to review the case for her. "Thanks for your help."

"You won't confront my boss, will you?" Kat said.

"Not without your permission. Is he bothering you, as well?"

"Me?" Kat laughed. "I'm not his type. Lucky me."

He waggled his pad. "Thanks."

He'd already uncovered one bit of data that had eluded Kirk, Hale mused as he returned to the car. Now he hoped it led somewhere in a hurry.

The desk officer informed Connie that Detective Crandall was out. "Care to leave a message?"

She tried to figure out what to write. *Saw a blue van. Intuition says it's important.* How idiotic. "I suppose not. Any idea when he'll be back?"

"I'm afraid not, Mrs. Simmons."

In the watch commander's office overlooking the counter, she caught sight of Joel. He was looking at her. His presence here proved he hadn't been driving the van, but she wasn't pleased when he reacted to their eye contact by getting to his feet.

Connie wasn't about to let him spook her. So she waited.

Reaching her, Joel gestured to an unoccupied nook in the lobby. "If you're filing more complaints about me, I'd like to hear 'em."

"Oh, for heaven's sake! That's not why I'm here." She might as well tell him, she supposed. "I saw a blue van near the store. It struck me as suspicious. I mean—"

"Suspicious in what way?"

She wasn't sure she should tell him there might be a witness to the food tampering. But then, Joel hadn't turned into a maniac who would hunt down an innocent onlooker. Besides, the van might be significant for completely unrelated reasons, such as a guy casing her store for a robbery.

Still, she wasn't certain how much to disclose. "It's probably my imagination," she temporized.

"Connie, I know someone's been giving you grief. It's not me and I'd like to prove it." Joel's voice came out ragged with emotion. "My career's on the line here. If you have any clue that could help, please tell me. Or tell the desk officer if you don't trust me. But I'd really like to get to the bottom of this."

A small thread of doubt wove through Connie's thoughts. This business of the blue van gave the first solid—well, not solid, but at least tentative—indication that someone else might be involved. And Joel sounded so genuinely worried.

Impulsively, she described what she'd observed. Including the van's presence on the day of the food tampering, and the Montana license plate.

"Montana," he repeated. "That rings a bell."

His statement surprised her. "It does?"

"You should repeat this to the captain."

She hadn't intended to make a formal report. Nevertheless, she let Joel escort her down the hall to the detective bureau.

Her ex did look kind of snappy in his uniform, she noted idly. As if from a great distance, she recalled why she'd once found him attractive. She recalled also that he was generally a decent man. "If I've been wrong about you, Joel, I'm sorry."

He answered slowly. "At least you're here now. That might help." In what must have been a painful concession, he added, "I had no business threatening you that day at Hale's. That was stupid and I apologize."

"Apology accepted."

They reached the captain's office. Joel explained the situation to the captain and departed.

Despite Frank Ferguson's customary air of cordiality, Connie had occasionally caught an edge of hostility aimed in her direction. She attributed it to the fact that, like all too many police officers, he'd suffered through a divorce. So she was glad when he called in Detective Tenille to listen to her information again. When she finished, Ferguson asked whether she had friends or family in Montana.

"No," she assured him.

"Former boyfriends, there or here?"

"No to that, too."

"Mrs. Simmons, have you dated anyone recently?" Frank asked as Kirk watched them uncertainly.

She didn't care for the personal nature of the inquiry. "Detective Tenille already covered that subject during our interview." Which, she recalled abruptly, had occurred *before* she and Hale became lovers. "Besides, my personal life is only relevant if there's a possibility the other person might be behind this, and there isn't!"

"Why is that, Mrs. Simmons?" the captain growled.

"Because Hale Crandall doesn't drive a blue van!" she shot back. "If you want further information about my love life, I suggest you get it from him, because unless you plan to arrest me, I'm done here."

She grabbed her purse. Frank waved his hand to stop her from bolting. "My apologies if I upset you. I have an idea who might be driving that van, but since you didn't get the plate number, I thought it wise to rule out other motives before we jump to conclusions."

She released a long breath. "Who is it?"

"I'm not at liberty to say. But if you see the van again, call 911 immediately."

"I'll do that." Barely containing her annoyance, she stalked out. In her opinion, the man's attitude toward women left a lot to be desired.

Well, she'd done her best. As her mood cooled, however, a scary thought struck Connie.

If Joel was innocent, the person in the blue van might be way more dangerous than she'd imagined. Fearful for her staff, she dialed the number at the shop and waited impatiently while it rang.

* * *

The housing development, named Amber View because the buildings reflected the characteristic brown of the dry summer landscape, had been built within the past few years. Proud homeowners did their best to compensate for the immature trees and surrounding brown hills with flower beds as vibrant as Connie's, Hale noted.

He'd been trying not to think about her all morning. Last night's declaration that they were finished had stunned him. He longed to believe she hadn't meant it. Perhaps she'd blurted the remark without thinking, he'd tried to tell himself during a restless night. Then again, shouldn't he have expected her withdrawal? Maybe she was just living down to her reputation of not supporting her man when he got caught up in the conflicts of police work.

Only, he didn't believe the picture Joel had painted of Connie. She was far more complicated and loving than that. Still, he doubted anything he could say would change her mind. He'd have to rely on their connection through Skip and the passage of time to present a second chance. Wrapping up this case ought to help, which made it more urgent than ever to find the real perp.

Turning his attention to locating the house, Hale wished he'd been able to call ahead. Without advance warning, Laura Niven, fearing it could be the bar owner, might ignore his knock.

He found it, just as Kat had described. At his knock, the door was opened by a middle-aged woman with a wary expression.

He displayed his badge and introduced himself. "Your daughter may have information about a case I'm investigating. It concerns a patron at the tavern."

"Please, Detective. Come in."

A pretty blonde in her early twenties materialized in the living room. While Hale explained his mission, her mother discreetly left them alone.

"Is this officer handsome?" Laura asked. "His name is kind of like Joe but not quite. Joey or… Joel, that's it!"

He nodded. "He gave you a card?"

"Yeah, right in front of my boss, who'd have been furious if I kept it. I tossed it in the trash. Kind of sorry, actually."

"Your boss saw you toss it?"

"Yes, I made a point of letting him see. So

he wouldn't think I was betraying him, or something. A real sicko."

Perhaps, Hale thought, the fellow had retrieved the card out of jealousy, although that would hardly explain the attacks on Connie's Curios.

Tenille's report hadn't considered the tavern owner as a possible perp, but then, Kirk hadn't known the man's history of annoying women or his apparent attraction to blondes. Could there be a prior connection to Connie? "Who emptied the trash?"

"Kat usually does it." A puzzled frown crossed her face. "Wait. There *was* a customer who said he'd lost a piece of paper. He asked me to bring him the wastebasket to search for it."

Unusual behavior, Hale reflected. "Did he find what he was looking for? Did he show it you?"

"He found whatever it was, but he didn't show it to me. He seemed kind of smug, though. Like he'd scored something valuable."

Since she might have confused the day or juxtaposed unrelated incidents, he walked her through the entire story. She described the stranger as heavyset, sixtyish and of medium height. He'd been drinking at the bar with friends when Laura disposed of the card. Minutes later, while it still lay in the trash, he'd precipitated a nasty quarrel with Joel.

An adrenaline jolt hit Hale. "Go on."

"I thought Joel might deck him. I'm glad he stopped, because the old guy had this pasty complexion. Like he wasn't well," she said.

"Then what happened?"

"He drove off. Then Joel left, but then the old guy returned and told me he'd lost a piece of paper. I figured he must be real forgetful, because when he went out again, he forgot his keys. He'd set them on the bar." Laura didn't appear to find that behavior unusual. "I figured I'd do him a favor, so I went after him."

"Do you recall what kind of car he drove?"

"He was standing in front of a blue van, searching his pockets." Laura wrinkled her nose. "He snatched the keys and didn't even thank me. I'm almost sorry I helped."

"I'm grateful you did," Hale told her.

When she mentioned that the van had Montana plates, that confirmed Hale's conclusion.

He assured her she'd done a great job and requested that she call if she remembered anything else. Excited, he phoned Frank Ferguson from the car.

The captain took the disclosure in stride.

"We just received a report of a suspicious blue van with Montana plates seen earlier cruising past Connie's shop." The captain explained that it had driven away. "I'm putting out an APB."

Amber View lay a mile or so past the strip of stores where Connie's Curios was located. "I'll swing by in case he's returned."

"Use extreme caution," the captain said. "We have to assume he's armed.

"Yeah. That occurred to me."

Norm Kinsey, the disgraced former lieutenant with whom Joel had argued weeks ago, might well have brought an agenda with him to Villazon: revenge on the man who'd testified against him. Harassing Connie had been merely a means to destroy Joel's career.

What good luck for Norm to have found the card. But no doubt he'd have invented some other way to point the finger.

As for the blaze in Ben's apartment, Norm could be the man Mrs. Rios had observed. Hale doubted the fire had been intended to cause such serious damage; more likely just to summon firefighters so they'd discover the planted drugs. He didn't understand the beef with Chief Lyons, who'd joined the force after the lieutenant got booted, but the implication that the chief's son was using drugs *had* succeeded in embarrassing the whole department.

Norm hadn't shrunk from arson or from endangering innocent customers who might be allergic to nuts. If the van had returned, Norm meant to strike again, and with each attack the danger increased.

Hale peeled out of the development and sped toward the gift shop.

Chapter Sixteen

In the July sunshine, the shopping center appeared normal. People came and went, a supermarket clerk collected scattered carts, and a compact bus bearing the name of an assisted living center was pulling away from the front of the gift store.

Hale's brain superimposed the earlier scene when he'd arrived to find light bars flashing and a policeman guarding the premises. No place was truly secure, no matter how serene the facade. Someone had reported seeing Norm's van here today. Even if the man had departed without causing mischief, he would return all too soon.

And do what? Hale wished he knew. He rolled along an aisle of parked cars, his window lowered. Shades of blue dotted the sea of whites, beiges and silvers. Cars, SUVs, station wagons. Why did blue have to be such a popular color?

He didn't spot Connie's maroon sedan, although presumably she was at work today. Whatever happened, she might get caught in the middle.

Hale chastised himself for focusing too much on the details and ignoring the big picture. The question of *who* had been harassing Connie mattered far less than the threat to her. Excessive loyalty to his old friend Joel had blinded him to what mattered most.

Well, he could still set things straight. Had to stay alert to accomplish that, though.

There! A blue van with Montana plates swerved toward the shop from around the edge of the building. Norm must have been watching for his chance, waiting for the elderly folks to leave. Despite the awkward angle, the hunch of the driver's shoulders and angry jut of his jaw were clearly recognizable.

The van slowed as it came abreast of the shop. Thanks to the reflection in the display glass, Hale noticed the downward slide of the passenger window.

Damn! Norm intended to hurl something. A Molotov cocktail or firebomb could set the entire store ablaze. Hale's pulse rate rocketed as he remembered all those display shelves full of hats, T-shirts, paper goods, electronics—fuel for an inferno.

He had to protect Connie. Had to stop the guy fast, even if it cost him his badge. Or his life. He couldn't afford to wait.

Drawing his gun, Hale rolled his car alongside the van, counting on the upward trajectory to prevent the bullets from hitting anyone inside the shop. Taking aim proved far trickier than those choreographed stunts on TV, and as he did, Norm Kinsey's pale eyes locked on his.

Hale shouted a command to halt and exit the vehicle. In response, a sneer twisted the older man's lips and into view flashed what appeared to be either an oversize pistol or oddly shaped rifle.

Hale fired. Amid a deafening explosion, the bullet clipped Norm's roof.

The van spun away. He'd prevented Norm from attacking the store, but the guy was escaping.

As Hale reversed course, he kept track of the van. It screeched in an arc and swerved for another pass. Not at the store, this time, but at him.

Surely the guy no longer believed his actions would reflect on Joel. Why didn't he simply flee?

Because he's got it in for me, too. Hale had seconded Joel's testimony. Although he hadn't witnessed the beating, he'd observed the prisoner's injuries. Also, Norm appeared to prefer going out in a blaze of glory. He zoomed toward Hale, his weapon aimed directly into the car.

Without time to roll up his window, Hale threw himself flat on the seat, causing a jolt of pain in his not-fully-healed left leg. The van peeled past amid a series of loud pops.

Hale felt a couple of sharp stings, and the spray of something wet and sticky and red.

Stalking toward the lobby, Connie nearly collided with Joel as he emerged from the lunchroom, cup of coffee in hand.

"Sorry," she muttered.

"What's eating you?" He shook a few drops from his hand.

"The captain has an attitude problem,"

Connie grumbled. "He pried into my private life as if I must have brought this on myself."

"You mean he found out you're sleeping with Hale?" Joel sniped.

She felt like kicking him. "Why don't you say that a little louder? Maybe somebody in the department didn't hear you."

Joel glanced around sheepishly. "Sorry. Didn't mean to shoot my mouth off. Especially as you may have just pulled my butt out of a sling," he said. "So what did Frank say? I mean, aside from nosing into your personal life."

"He said he has an idea who owns the van, but he wouldn't share it with me." Connie hated being left in the dark. "Who do *you* think it is?"

Without hesitation he said, "Norm Kinsey. He moved to Montana, but I ran into him at Jose's Tavern a few weeks back."

She recognized the name. How could she forget, when the investigation into the lieutenant's beating of a prisoner had stressed out her husband so badly? "He has no right to hold a grudge. All you did was testify about what you'd seen."

"People like him don't accept responsibility. Easier to blame me for losing his job and his pension," Joel said. "He had plenty of support in the department, too. A number of his old pals have since retired, but there are those who *still* wouldn't mind seeing me get railroaded."

"I wish you'd told me about this," Connie said, appalled. "I didn't have a clue." While she wouldn't have acceded to his demand for a baby or abandoned her shop, she might have been more willing to ride out their difficulties had she known of the hostility he faced at work.

"Wives are supposed to stand by their husbands," Joel answered tightly.

"And husbands are supposed to cherish their wives," she retorted. "Guess we both messed up."

They fell silent as a couple of officers passed in the corridor. Although the men barely glanced at them, Connie suspected the whole department would shortly be abuzz with speculation.

"I suppose we were always oil and water. Or fire and ice. Stuff that doesn't mix." Despite the impression that he was addressing his cup of coffee, Joel apparently meant the words for her. "Guess it's time I moved on, although I doubt I'll find another lady as classy as you. After the way you spoke up today, I'm done blaming you for the breakup."

"Thanks for the compliment." She hadn't received one from him since the early months of their marriage.

"What compliment?"

"You called me 'classy.'"

"It's the truth." Joel heaved a reluctant sigh. "You bowled me over from the start. The way you dressed, the way you walked, the whole shot. Guess I didn't know how to treat you once I had you."

Out of the blue, she felt liberated from the weight of his resentment. "No hard feelings?"

"I don't promise to draw smiley faces on the alimony checks," he muttered. "But I'm willing to bury the hatchet."

"Me, too."

They shook hands. What an unexpected development, Connie thought. Until a short while ago, she'd considered Joel her worst enemy. Now he might someday even become a friend.

She was about to leave when someone shouted Joel's name along with a code she didn't recognize. Abruptly Joel changed from cordial to tense, and he took off at a lope.

Outside, sirens wailed. "What's happening?" Connie asked the desk officer when she reached the lobby.

"It's an officer requesting assistance," he said.

That usually meant an officer was in trouble, sometimes dire trouble, Connie knew. "Who is it?" *Please, not Rachel. And please not—*

"Hale Crandall," he answered.

Connie struggled to catch her breath. She could hardly take it in. And in that stunned moment, she saw what a terrible mistake she'd made. She'd been ready to cast the man aside because he wouldn't choose her over his pals, when he'd only been behaving according to his sense of fairness and his sense of what was right—in this case, Joel's innocence.

Whereas she'd been judgmental and stubborn. And totally out of touch with her own heart.

Connie prayed he was all right. However much of himself, of his time, Hale was willing to spare, she wanted it.

Only, she might have made that discovery too late.

Hale stared in disbelief at the sticky mess of red. Paintballs! Potentially damaging if they struck a person's eye; otherwise harmless. Norm had risked his life for this?

No—for the points. For the pleasure of landing the last blow. Unless, of course, he escaped long enough to continue seeking revenge.

Disgusted, Hale radioed for assistance, then started forward, but the van had swung onto the street and was picking up speed. Although a siren sounded, it came from the wrong direction.

On the radio, Hale reported his status. He was seeking a gap in the traffic flow when, ahead of him, the van wavered wildly for no apparent reason. It cut across a lane of traffic and veered back into the parking lot.

For a moment, he feared Norm planned another rush at the store. Possibly Norm carried a second weapon and had used the paintballs as a diversion.

The van crashed into a light post and crunched to a halt. The motor sputtered into silence. Hale drove through the parking lot toward the van, aware that this might be a trap, although a peculiar one. Still, perhaps the man believed he had nothing to lose.

His left side smarted as he got out, gun drawn, keeping a line of cars between him and the suspect. He could see Norm slumped over the wheel. No smell of gasoline, Hale noted with relief, since a broken gas line meant an imminent fire hazard.

A black-and-white veered off the road and shrilled to a stop, followed by a paramedic unit and a second cruiser. At last, backup.

The patrolmen and Hale closed in, still receiving no reaction from Norm. Pasty-gray, he scarcely appeared to be breathing. They darted forward, yanked open the door and snapped on the cuffs.

Bloodshot eyes drifted open. "Guess the ticker got me before you did, huh, boy?" he gasped. "Gave you bastards a run for your money."

"You figured you were dying anyway?" Hale demanded.

"Got scores to settle before I go." The man groaned.

"Yeah, you terrorized an innocent woman and child. What a brave legacy!" Hale snapped. "And why single out Ben Lyons? What'd he or his father do to you?"

A grimace. "Say what?"

A paramedic intervened to remove Norm for treatment. "You should get yourself looked at, too," the fellow advised Hale.

"Not necessary." With the adrenaline draining, a couple of steps sent agony through his leg. He wanted to check on Connie though. He just had to reach the store.

Another effort and his ankle buckled. Hale fell onto the pavement hands-first.

"Over here!" the paramedic called to his colleagues. "The detective's lost a lot of blood."

"It's only paint." But his protest got lost in the fuss. Submitting to the inevitable, Hale stayed put, mostly because he doubted he could walk.

With tremendous strength of will, Connie hid her fears while collecting Skip and driving him to Keri's house. She didn't dare turn on the car radio or call anyone for news, either.

If the worst *had* happened, better to delay until Dr. Federov could help her explain to the boy. And if Hale had escaped harm, Connie didn't want to cause her son panic unnecessarily.

She said nothing to Skip or Keri, merely wished them a good day and promised to return after work as usual. Aware that they were watching, she walked to the car at a measured pace.

Inside, she called Hale's cell phone. She listened to the ring and nearly screamed aloud at the customer-not-available message.

Now what? Go back to the police station? Call Joel and find out what he'd learned? She put the car in gear as she struggled to reach a decision. On emerging from the area where Keri lived, she caught sight of emergency vehicles cramming the lot by her store. A paramedic van wailed off, leaving two black-and-whites.

The incident had occurred *here?* Her stomach clenching, Connie stopped beside a young patrolman, Bill Norton. "Is Hale okay?"

He glanced up. "A lot of blood. They took him to the med center. That's all I know. You might ask over there." He indicated an officer taking measurements on the pavement near where a blue van was smashed against a light post. A blue van with Montana plates.

So she'd been correct about the threat. But she'd never suspected the danger would involve Hale instead of her.

She got out of her sedan on shaky knees. Tracy Johnson finished interviewing an officer and headed her way, camera case slung over one shoulder and tape recorder in hand.

"Looks like they caught your stalker," the

reporter announced. "Crandall to the rescue again! That guy ought to wear a superhero costume."

Connie didn't find the lighthearted reference amusing. "How badly was he hurt?"

The shorter woman blinked in surprise. "Oh, he just reinjured his leg."

Incredible news, almost too good to believe. "You're sure?"

"Yeah. I got an exclusive interview." Tracy chuckled. "He sure looks a mess, though! Norm Kinsey shot him with a red paintball."

Not blood—a paintball. "They took him to the hospital?"

"Yeah, as a precaution. But he's in a lot better shape than Kinsey."

Connie sagged against her car. "I thought he'd been shot."

"Norm? Heart attack, they told me."

"No, Hale! I was petrified." Immediately, she regretted revealing that much. "Like I told you, he's my next-door neighbor."

Tracy smiled. "More than that, I'm guessing. But don't worry. The *Voice* doesn't print gossip. Hey, can I get a reaction quote about what's happened? I mean, you *were* the target."

On the point of demurring, Connie recalled

that this meant publicity for the store. "I'm grateful to the Villazon police and especially Detective Crandall." After a moment, she added, "My staff and customers have been tremendously loyal throughout. I appreciate their support."

"Want to comment on Lieutenant Kinsey and his actions?"

Connie quelled her impulse to call him a slug. "I'm sorry for his family and friends, if he has any, because I guess he's in bad shape. But I'm glad my employees and I are safe from him now."

"Great." Tracy clicked off the recorder. "See you soon!" She dashed off. This being Monday, her deadline loomed in a few hours.

Connie navigated a path to the store, her relief yielding to self-criticism. With the worst fears soothed, she had the uncomfortable leisure to examine her mistakes.

Hale had accused her of abandoning Joel—an unfair charge—yet in a sense that was what she'd done to Hale. She'd rejected him for supporting her ex's innocence, when all along he'd been right. She hadn't believed in him enough to hold on until things were worked out. Had it been because she was just too afraid of repeating her disappointments with her father and her husband? If only she'd dared to take the risk!

Although aching for the closeness with Hale she'd sacrificed, Connie assumed a pleasant expression for Jo Anne and Paris, who greeted her with whoops of excitement.

"You should have seen Hale!" Jo Anne declared. "He practically saved the store single-handedly."

"It was a Wild West show," added her daughter. "I'm glad he's all right." The officers had questioned them as witnesses and told them his condition, they explained. Then, speaking over each other, the pair proceeded to describe the confrontation.

"I'm glad Joel's in the clear," Jo Anne admitted when they'd completed the tale. "I always figured he'd get his act together one of these days, and now maybe he will."

Connie agreed. But her thoughts weren't on her ex-husband, but rather on Hale. Was it possible she'd lost his trust forever?

She had no idea how to win him back. But she intended to try.

Chapter Seventeen

That afternoon, Hale lost count of how many people described him as a hero. The staff at the hospital, who braced the ankle and put him on crutches; the media, who peppered him with questions outside the police station, where he'd gone right after the hospital released him and Derek Reed. Wait—Derek didn't count. As public relations officer, it was his job to exaggerate for the press.

In the department, Chief Lyons pumped Hale's hand gratefully. "I can't tell you how much this means to me. Personally as well as professionally."

"Norm didn't confess to starting the fire," Hale reminded him.

"I don't see how the D.A. can ignore the connection," the chief replied. "Two nearly simultaneous attempts to frame people in order to disgrace the department. That's hard to dismiss."

Hale hoped so. As for Norm, he'd lost the opportunity to provide a further statement. The heart attack had proved fatal. He'd died at the medical center.

As Hale gathered papers at his desk to prepare for a medical leave that dovetailed with the Fourth of July holiday, a couple of veterans who'd closed ranks against Joel entered the detective bureau. He braced for their anger, but instead they apologized and offered a handshake.

"We figured Norm got a bum rap," explained a sergeant who'd previously maintained that the prisoner probably deserved a beating. "Terrorizing Connie to get revenge on Joel goes way over the top."

"He dishonored us," his comrade added. "We're supposed to be the good guys."

After they dispersed Joel also had kind words. "You stuck by me again, buddy. I owe you plenty."

"A dozen doughnuts ought to cover it." Hale poured himself coffee from the pot in the lunchroom.

Joel fetched sugar and cream, sparing Hale a couple of painful hops. "We owe a debt to Connie, too. If she hadn't stopped by to report the van, you might not have nabbed him."

So that's where the tip had originated. "She came in personally?"

"Yeah, we were talking. I had to run off after we got your 'officer assist,'" Joel confirmed. "I guess she must have been plenty upset."

"Devastated," Hale acknowledged, though in truth, he hadn't heard from her. But then, he'd switched off his cell phone after some clown in the press got hold of the number and refused to take "no interviews" for an answer. He could have called *her,* obviously, but first he had to decide how to present his case. He no longer trusted proximity and their fundamental attraction to bring them together.

Too bad he wasn't a candlelight-and-violins kind of fellow. He needed another plan to woo her, something suitable for a man who really cared.

A short while later, inspiration struck.

* * *

As she drove up, the sight of huge mounds of dirt in her front yard alarmed Connie. A swarm of gophers couldn't have done a more thorough job of devastating the flower bed. In this case, however, the damage clearly resulted from the commands of a single large, insane gopher who stood on crutches directing a gardener.

A light breeze ruffled Hale's hair and dirt smeared his cheek. Today she'd agonized over this wonderful man nearly to the point of despair. And now he was destroying her landscaping?

"Are they digging us a swimming pool?" Skip asked hopefully.

"I believe Hale's digging his own grave," Connie muttered before remembering with chagrin that he'd had a real brush with death earlier. "I can't imagine what they're doing," she amended.

She'd furnished a simplified explanation of the day's events to Skip when she picked him up. He'd been thrilled to learn that Hale had conquered the candy bar villain.

Once they stopped, Skip ran across the grass. "Hi! I'm sorry you got hurt again. What're you doing?"

"Planting." Hale glanced past the boy to Connie. "I'd do it myself, but the doc says no heavy labor."

"Besides, I gotta earn a living," said the gardener who regularly cut Connie's grass.

As Connie joined them, she saw the poor flowers clumped to one side. Hale followed her gaze. "No problem. We'll replant them around the base when we're done."

"What *is* this?' she demanded.

He indicated three plastic tubs containing rosebushes. The attached color photos showed a range of pink shades—her favorite color.

"An ordinary guy would buy you a dozen roses and in a couple of days, they'd wind up in the trash," Hale explained as the gardener resumed enlarging the holes. "I'm giving you flowers that'll last for years. Plus, the bushes should keep ball-playing clodzillas from trampling your lawn."

I'm fond of those ball-playing clodzillas, she nearly replied. Still, his high-handedness rankled. "You aren't simply *giving* them to me. You made an executive decision to tear up my property without consulting me."

Hale's mouth dropped open, then twitched into a rueful smile. "Typical me, huh? Good intentions, bad execution."

His crestfallen expression dissolved Connie's indignation. If not for their audience, she'd have thrown her arms around the man and hugged him, dirt and all.

"I'm sure I'll enjoy them," she managed.

"I promise to help with the pruning."

Before Connie could frame a response, Skip tugged at Hale's shirt. "Let's go swimming!"

"Have to wait a day or so, since I'm an invalid again." His expression brightened. "If your mom's still speaking to me, let's hold a Fourth of July pool party. You can invite your little friends, I'll bring mine and we'll swim all day."

"Yay!"

"But first, look at this." Hale indicated the wickedly sharp thorns on one of the bushes. "These can stab. Watch out for them."

Skip stuck his hands in his pockets as if for protection. "Okay."

Hale turned to Connie. "I hope you two will eat with me tonight. I picked up dinner. My place okay?"

"Fabulous. And Hale…thanks." She regretted snapping at him, even though the mess in her yard *had* been upsetting. "For the roses.

For catching that jerk Kinsey. And mostly for not getting killed."

"The pleasure is definitely mine." He checked his watch. "We should be done here in half an hour. Meet you at my place."

She changed clothes while Skip played in his room. When they emerged, the restored annuals covered the bare legs of the rosebushes, and the earth had been tamped neatly around them.

A lasting gift, far more meaningful than a bouquet, as Hale had said. Connie couldn't believe she'd given the man so much trouble in the past. His boisterousness and occasional missteps paled in comparison to his generosity and steadfastness.

When she and Skip strolled into his house, Connie noticed that someone had run a vacuum cleaner recently. Also, with the cabinet doors replaced, the kitchen looked downright respectable. She was impressed.

As they ate the lasagna and pickle ice cream Hale had picked up, he detailed the day's events, depicting the confrontation as a grand adventure. Skip was enthralled.

He also mentioned the apology he'd received from the veterans who'd supported Norm, which reminded Connie of her conversation with her ex. “Joel and I raised the white flag,” she told him. “Hale, I had no idea half the department sided against him for testifying. He should have told me.”

“Real men don’t whine about their problems.” With a napkin, he wiped pickle juice from Skip’s chin.

“If he had—” She stopped. That hadn’t been the only problem with their marriage. “Now that I know the truth, I can sympathize. And I’m sorry I didn’t trust your instincts about him. I guess in a lot of ways you knew him better than I did.”

“Hey, I didn’t see the side of him who punched his fist through the wall and totaled one of your vases,” Hale conceded. “You had reason to be cautious.”

“Maybe so, but I was wrong about a lot of things.”

“Let’s talk about this later.”

She heard an undercurrent of seriousness in his voice, which sent a shivery feeling through her. “Of course.”

Skip kept them occupied for the rest of the evening. When at last the little boy was tucked into bed and asleep, Connie and Hale moved to her den. He plopped his feet on the coffee table without removing his shoes. She might have reproved him, except that Skip had already gouged it with his toys. Then Hale jumped right in.

"I've been reviewing you and me," he said. "Guess I ought to find out where I stand. Still in the doghouse?"

"No. Completely forgiven. I hope I am, too." Rosebushes notwithstanding, she wondered where *she* stood with him.

"Glad we're back to normal."

What was normal? Friends who also happened to be lovers? That no longer seemed enough to Connie, but maybe Hale still wasn't ready for more. Besides, she hadn't forgotten how she'd anguished over him, how she'd decided to take him on whatever terms he wanted.

Hale was here now. Connie would make the best of that.

"You're not the only one who's been reviewing you and me," she said. "I'm willing to work out an arrangement that keeps us together without asking too much of you."

His usually expressive eyes looked sleepy. "You won't impose on my lifestyle, right?"

"Exactly." Connie interlaced her fingers. "Since I realize you probably aren't interested in getting married—"

"Absolutely not," Hale drawled. "I'd drive you crazy doing stuff like throwing parties and digging up your yard."

"I'd drive *you* crazy," she countered. "Fussing over the decor and deep-cleaning the kitchen."

He nodded. "The first time I met you, I said to myself, there's an incredibly sexy woman, but we'd make each other miserable because she likes those froufrou ceramic figurines." A quick afterthought: "Plus, you'd hate my black satin sheets."

A tremor ran through Connie. A shudder—or anticipation? "You have black satin sheets?"

"I don't expect you to sleep on them. Although they're really soft and your blond hair would look fabulous spread on the pillow. Used to be one of my fantasies," he noted.

A longing seized her to share that fantasy. "We might try them out."

"We also can't get married because I've been in love with you for years, and if Joel figures out that I coveted you before the divorce, he might act ugly. Like, mess with your candy bars."

"Joel wouldn't do that!" She blushed. "As you've been telling me for weeks." In the ensuing pause, she finally heard the words that had slipped past her. "You're in love with me?"

"But none of that wedding nonsense," Hale murmured. "You'd sashay down the aisle in a gorgeous gown and I'd stand at the altar with food spilled on my tuxedo and my pants ripped."

Connie laughed in spite of herself. "Probably by one of those rosebushes!"

"There's also the question of when." He took her hands in his. "I'd push for August or September. You'd insist on a romantic June wedding, which would mean waiting a whole year."

Her heart rate speed up. "I already had one fancy wedding, and that didn't turn out so well. A simple ceremony will be fine."

She paused, startled by her words. They were discussing marriage as if it might actually happen.

"Is there something you want to ask me?" she murmured.

When Hale met her gaze, love shone in his eyes. "As a matter of fact, yes. Ready?"

"As ready as I'll ever be." She scarcely dared to breathe.

"Will you marry me?"

Connie nearly floated off the couch. "Finally!" she burst out.

"I'm interpreting that as a yes." Hale said wryly.

She touched his cheek, relishing the end-of-day stubble. "Seeing you become a daddy to Skip helped me recognize how often you've been here for me. I'm not even certain when I fell in love."

"I'll settle for five minutes ago," he returned. "As long as you love me now."

What a dear comment! "You're a very special man, Hale. Did you know that you're my—"

"Stop!"

"What?"

"If anyone else calls me a hero, I'm chucking my badge."

"I was about to say that you're my best friend," Connie corrected sweetly.

He gathered her for a kiss. A very long and satisfying kiss. When they came up for air, she rested against him contentedly.

Hale's voice rumbled through her. "Would you mind if I keep my house for parties and guests and general mayhem?"

Why not? "Sounds like a plan. Besides, Skip loves the swimming pool."

He hummed with pleasure. "As for what's left of your china knickknacks, you should keep them in case we have a little princess of our own."

Joy swelled inside Connie. "She might be a tomboy."

"Even better." He kicked off his shoes, which slid across the coffee table and clunked to the floor. "You don't mind my wanting more children?"

Connie ignored the urge to correct his behavior. "Not as long as it's a team effort."

"Oh, we're having a whole team?"

The only way to end this conversation, she decided, was to kiss him again. So she did. And again and again until they moved into the bedroom.

If she owned black satin sheets, life would be perfect. But Connie had a feeling they'd get around to those very soon indeed.

And, if she had anything to say about it, often.

* * * * *